FEELINGS RUN DEEP

FEELINGS RUN DEEP

CALLIE HART™ BOOK THREE

RENÉE JAGGÉR

This book is a work of fiction. All of the characters, organizations, and events portrayed in this novel are either products of the author's imagination or are used fictitiously. Sometimes both.

Copyright © 2020 Renée Jaggér
Cover by Cover by Fantasy Book Design
Cover copyright © LMBPN Publishing

LMBPN Publishing supports the right to free expression and the value of copyright. The purpose of copyright is to encourage writers and artists to produce the creative works that enrich our culture.

The distribution of this book without permission is a theft of the author's intellectual property. If you would like permission to use material from the book (other than for review purposes), please contact support@lmbpn.com. Thank you for your support of the author's rights.

LMBPN Publishing
PMB 196, 2540 South Maryland Pkwy
Las Vegas, NV 89109

Version 1.01, September 2020
eBook ISBN: 978-1-64971-151-9
Print ISBN: 978-1-64202-945-1

A month after we returned from Paris, Sam and I went back to the loft to find a note from our landlord taped to the door. It was an envelope, really, taped just above the doorknob with our names handwritten on the outside. I took it down with a frown before sliding the key into the lock. "Did you forget to pay the rent again, Sam?"

"Me? No way." Sam adjusted the lime-green blazer they had put on for our outing. It clashed with the neon-pink ball cap in my opinion, but somehow the two colors worked when they wore them together. They had a look all their own, which made them easy to pick out of a crowd at least.

We went through the door, and I closed it behind us, then dropped the envelope on the table and sat down. Sam immediately took the seat across from me. We eyed each other, possibilities for what the letter might be about running through our heads. As far as I could tell, we had paid the rent on time, and it wasn't time for us to renew the lease yet. Maybe one of the neighboring apartments had a bug infestation. That had happened once before, and we'd had to clear out for a week while they fumigated the whole building. Not fun, but not the worst thing that could happen in a rented loft.

"Well?" Sam leaned on their fist. "You going to open it, or should I?"

I thought back to the last time I had put off opening an important document and decided, "I'll open it."

I slid my finger under the flap and pulled out a single-page typed letter on the building's letterhead. Uh-oh. That was never good.

"Well?" Sam repeated after I'd had a moment to scan the letter. "What does it say?"

My heart sank to my toes. "They sold the building, Sam."

"What? They can't do that without some sort of consent or notification or…something! Let me see that." Sam seized the letter from my grasp, their eyes shifting back and forth as they read the same news I'd just gotten. "It says here they plan to demolish the building!"

"Yep," I said.

"And we have thirty days to find a new place?"

"That's what it says."

Sam crumpled the letter and bounced it against the wall with a snarl. "Are you kidding me? Callie, we'll never find a place this size that we can afford! Well, maybe you will, but me? I'm living on scholarship money. I don't know how I'm going to get together a deposit, let alone cover an increase in rent. God, I might have to get a *job*! Then my grades will go into the toilet, and I'll lose my scholarship, and then I'll have to pick up a second job just to cover tuition. I would have to kiss my social life goodbye, and I'm *so* not doing that."

"Sam." I reached across the table to put my hand over theirs. "It'll be okay."

"That's easy for you to say." Sam pulled their hand away. "You could pay twice the rent as this place and still have money to burn with what Ronan's paying you."

That wasn't true. Ronan paid me well as his bodyguard, sure, but I had my expenses, and taxes to pay. Rent and monthly expenses didn't put me in the poorhouse, but if I had to double my rent without finding additional income, it would make things tight.

"Look, it'll be fine. We'll look at some online rental ads before I go to work in a few hours. This is a college town, and Columbus is a big city. There are bound to be afford-able rentals somewhere in the area, right?" I snagged my laptop from the coffee table and brought it back, powering it on.

Sam sighed. "I guess. Good thing I grabbed a paper." They tossed the wadded-up newspaper on the table. Sam had been planning to use it as part of an art project they'd been working on, not to read it, but a little smoothing out, and it was as good as new.

Over the next two hours, Sam scoured the newspaper, then online websites looking for housing that met all our parameters. First of all, it had to have at least two bedrooms and plenty of living space. Since Sam and I didn't want to share a bathroom, it also needed two of those. Two-bed, two-bath apartments were easy enough to find, but not within the price range we needed to hit. The few that did match our query were in bad neighborhoods where crime was high, or else out in the suburbs. That was too far of a commute for Sam, who took the bus or public transit to school whenever I couldn't drop them off. With my unpredictable work schedule, that was happening more often than not this semester.

We found a few that ticked all the boxes for us, but when I called to inquire, the landlord told us the places had already been rented, or that they wouldn't be available until August. That was the biggest problem with renting in a college town—most leases went from August to July. Finding decent housing on short notice at this time of year was going to be a crapshoot.

Sam groaned and leaned back from their computer, popping their neck. "It's no use. We're in the middle of a semester. All the housing that's posted isn't even available until next fall. That or it's too expensive, or just wrong. I wish they'd told us they were going to sell the building. Then you could've bought it."

I frowned at Sam. Never mind that I didn't want to be a landlord and didn't know the first thing about it since I couldn't possibly have afforded it. It was a moot point anyway since that wasn't what'd happened. We'd been blindsided by bad news, and now all we could do was scramble to salvage our lives in the aftermath.

I glanced around the loft, which felt more like a home now than anywhere else I'd lived. Sam's paintings hung on the walls. I knew where everything was and where it should go, even things we hadn't gotten around to purchasing yet. Sam and I could've lived in that loft together forever and never even minded paying the rent. Thirty days in the future, however, they were going to knock the building down. Every memory of everything that had happened there would be gone just like that.

What if we couldn't find a place in time? I supposed Sam might be able to find space in one of the dorms to finish out the semester, but what would I do? I might be able to find a smaller apartment I could afford, but it wouldn't be the same, living alone. I liked having Sam as a roommate and couldn't imagine life without them.

"We'll find a way to make it work." I turned back to Sam. "Don't worry about the deposit. I can cover it. And if we have to take a more expensive place, I'll cover more than half the rent. If I need to, I can ask Ronan for a raise."

"That wouldn't be fair," Sam said, sitting up again. "I can't ask you to do that, Callie. I joke, but I know you're not made of money."

An alarm went off on my phone, reminding me that it was time to get ready for my evening shift at Ronan's. I picked it up and sighed as I turned off the alarm. "I have to go to work. Maybe Ronan has some connections and can pull strings to help us."

"You think he will?"

I thought Ronan would do just about anything if I asked the right way, but that was beside the point. Ever since we'd come back from Paris, he'd been more at ease around me. We'd spent way too many of my days off together, walking around town or watching movies either at the loft or at his place. He'd been listening to me more about his personal security, too. Maybe it was the impending war with the vampires, or maybe it was something else. I'd begun to think there was a spark of something between us, but neither of us was ready to discuss that.

I shrugged. "Sure? Why not?"

A knock on the door made me almost jump out of my skin.

Sam twisted their neck around to frown at the door. "Maybe it's the landlord. I hope it is. He owes us an apology."

If it was the landlord, Sam would probably lose their temper, which meant I'd better answer the door. I was on my way out anyway. After a second knock, I tugged the door open and found a thin young woman with pointed ears and short hair waiting on the other side—another fae. I'd met plenty of them over the last two months, but she was the first one I'd ever seen with pointed ears.

I was so distracted by the ears, I didn't notice she was holding a letter out to me until she cleared her throat. "A courtesy from Queen Mab."

"Oh, right." I took the letter. "It's not going to bite me or anything, is it?"

She obviously didn't get the joke. The fae courier frowned and hurried away.

"What is it now?" Sam asked. "Are they going to take your car too?"

I shut the door and turned the letter over in my hand. "No. At least, I don't think so. It's from Mab." I opened the letter, just as I had the first. More bad news. "War," I said. "They've finally made it official."

"Who declared war on whom?"

"I don't think it matters," I said, lowering the letter.

Sam was out of their chair in an instant. "Of course it matters! If it was the fae, they'll be seen as the aggressors, and the vampires can claim whatever they do is in self-defense. History remembers two things about every war: who fired the first shot, and the day it ended. Everything in the middle is always a little fuzzy."

My phone rang, and I lifted it to see Ronan's smiling face on the screen. "I'm heading out," I answered.

He ignored me. "I just got a letter saying we're at war, Callie. You need to get here right away."

I shifted the phone so I could hold it between my ear and my shoulder while I grabbed my keys. "I just said I'm on my way. I was about to go out the door when you called."

"I don't mean just for work, Callie," Ronan said. "Pack a bag. I want you to stay with me until this is over."

I sighed into the phone. "Ronan—"

"You're an unaligned fae, Callie. That means you're in danger. The vampires will pick off all the easy targets first, and of all of them, you have the highest profile. Also, they know they can use you to get to me. I'm telling you, they'll come for you first. If something happened to you…I don't know how I'd live with myself. Please, Callie. This could be life or death."

My eyes shifted to Sam, still waiting pensively at the table. "What about Sam?"

"Yes, of course Sam can come. Both of you are always welcome here."

"Okay, I'll see you in thirty." I hung up and turned to my roommate. "Pack a bag, Sam. Ronan wants us to come stay with him for a few days."

If he had his way, we'd be staying there until the end of the war, which could be months or even years from now. His house was as close as you could get to a fae fortress on

Earth, and he wasn't wrong that Sam and I would be safer there than in our loft. Still, we couldn't just pick up our lives and move into his mansion. It would be weird living with my boss, and Sam still had classes to get to. That, and it would take us much longer than thirty minutes to pack up all our things. I didn't know if I could put together a week's worth of clothes in that time.

I certainly wasn't going to turn down an offer to stay in a tightly controlled fortress while war broke out, though. It was a better offer than I would have expected to get as an independent fae.

I pocketed my phone and stepped toward my bedroom to get packing, but paused when I noticed shadows moving outside the window. At first, I thought it might be birds. After all, we were several stories up. What else could it be? But the shadows seemed too large and moved wrong to be birds. Something else was out there.

My gun was in my bedroom, but I had to pass the windows to get there. Maybe I was overreacting, or the shadows could be playing tricks on me. It was hard to tell without looking outside, which I didn't want to do, at least not without my gun by my side. I took a deep breath and ran for it.

I was in front of the windows when the largest of them shattered and two vampires leapt through, tumbling onto the floor.

CHAPTER TWO

The vampires snarled at me and pawed at the shattered glass on the floor. They stood between me and my bedroom door, blocking any chance of me grabbing my gun. The one on the right lunged at me. I moved back and darted for the closest thing resembling a weapon I could find: one of the kitchen chairs. I held it out in front of me legs-first as the vampire leapt at me. He slashed at the chair legs with his claws, snapping them.

"Good idea," I said and smashed the chair against the floor. The seat portion broke after a second smack, and a twist left me with two makeshift wooden stakes. "One for each of you."

The vampires separated, trying to circle around to either side of me so I'd have to choose which one to fight and put my back to the other. They obviously hadn't heard I'd gotten better with my magic since Vaughn last saw me. Now that I didn't have to worry about cleaning the loft up to get my deposit back, I could let loose without worry. I blasted the one moving to my left with the strongest ice spell I could muster, but he jumped out the way before the blast hit him, and I wound up freezing one of Sam's portrait pieces on the wall instead.

The vampire on my right charged in, swiping his claws at me. I turned to fling a spell at him, but the other vampire lunged and I had a perfect shot. It just meant ignoring the other vampire closing in.

Sam shouted as they charged out of their room, a hockey stick raised. With a loud thwack, she smashed it into the vampire's head while I hit the other with another ice spell. Neither strike put the vampires down for the count, but the frozen one was now the lesser of my worries. I turned my back to him to help Sam with the other vampire.

He grabbed Sam's hockey stick, gripping the flat end of it and wrenching it so it snapped in half. Bad move, since that left Sam with a sharp wooden spear. I shouted and flung an ice spell at the vampire, forcing him to move or get frozen to the fridge. He leapt toward Sam, obviously not thinking. Sam thrust the spear straight through the vampire's chest.

One down, one to go.

We turned in unison to the one frozen to the wall between a Picasso-esque portrait by Sam and what I thought might be a stylized painting of a bee.

The vampire stopped struggling against the ice to grin at us and hiss through his bloody teeth. "Go on. Kill me. He'll still come for you. There's nowhere you can hide and be safe. Nowhere!"

"Good," I said. "I hope he does come because I'm going to sharpen a stake just for your boss. Make sure you save him a spot in Hell." I jammed both of my makeshift stakes into the vampire's chest.

He leaned into them, hissing and gurgling until he turned to dust.

I let go of the stakes, which clattered to the floor, then swiped my arm over my face. "Well, at least we don't have to clean the place up to get our deposit back if they're going to knock it down."

Two more vampires crashed through another window, and I heard the glass in my bedroom shatter too. No doubt at least one vampire was in there. I wanted to take them all on. The idea of vampires tainting my belongings by going through my stuff sparked a fire of rage in my chest that left me itching for a fight. However, as more glass broke and more vampires flooded into the apartment, it became clear that I couldn't take them all, not even with Sam's help.

"Callie!" Sam shouted and pointed at the door.

They were right. Running was the only option we had. We'd have to come back for our things, and when we did, I was going to stake every one of those bastards.

I grabbed my keys from the counter and ran for the door. The vampires raced after us and followed us into the hallway. I would have been worried about them finding and eating the other tenants if I didn't know the other loft on our floor was empty. Not every apartment in the building was empty, though, so I yanked the fire alarm handle down on my way to the stairs. That would put the elevators out of service, but at least everyone would get out of the building, and the fire department would show up to investigate. If they found a bunch of snarling, fanged beasts around, that was sure to make the news, and I was pretty sure Vaughn didn't want to be tonight's headline.

As the alarm screamed, the vampires flinched and raised their hands. They hissed at Sam and me as we ran to the stairs, but none dared to follow us.

We raced down the stairs just the same, sliding down banisters and hopping over and around the other tenants, much to their displeasure. Rather than file onto the sidewalk with everyone else, we went out the back to the parking lot.

"What now?" Sam asked as we jogged toward the car.

"Now we go to Ronan's and regroup," I said and tossed them the keys. "You drive. I'll keep an eye out for anyone following us."

The tradeoff for letting Sam drive was that I had to listen to their music, which was mostly thrash metal. I like headbanging music as much as anyone, but I also like to understand the lyrics. Apparently, that wasn't a requirement for Sam to enjoy a song; it just had to be loud.

After a single song, I convinced them I needed quiet to concentrate. I was tracking the license plates on cars as well as their makes and models in my head, trying to make sure none of them were Vaughn's vampires following us to Ronan's.

"You're bleeding," Sam said.

"Huh?"

"Your arm." They pointed.

I turned my arm over and noted a cut. Adrenaline had kept me from feeling whatever had happened, but I wasn't surprised. The vampires had been slashing and snapping at me, and I had been standing right next to the glass when they broke through. On closer inspection, I found several more small cuts and bruises, all on the side of my body that had been facing the window when they broke through. None of them were life-threatening or horribly painful… yet. Once the adrenaline wore off, though, I'd hurt like hell. Well, pain was good, as my drill sergeant used to say. It lets you know you're alive.

I beeped the gate at Ronan's and we pulled through, then I asked Sam to stop while I got out for a last look-see. I forgot the gate was made of iron, though, and pulled my hand away with a hiss after I grasped a bar. My palm was sporting two brand new blisters I'd have to wrap.

I sighed and chided myself. "You're falling apart, Callie."

I got back in, and we drove up the driveway. Mark met us at the front door, announcing that Ronan had called everyone in. The front room was crowded since all the security officers had brought their luggage in and set it down in favor of getting straight to work. The house was in the process of going into lockdown, which meant nobody would be allowed to come or go. The butler, housekeeper, and gardener were there, and mad as hell about not being able to return to their families.

Ronan raised his hands to calm the red-faced house-keeper. "I know your grandson's birthday is tomorrow, Edna," he said, "but you could be targeted. I would hate for that to happen while you were at his birthday party. Wouldn't you?"

She crossed her arms. "Why would they target me? I'm not even fae."

"They'll target anyone close to Ronan to get to him," I said. "That's how they work. They know they can't get to us here, so they'll wait until they can pick people off on the outside, whittling us down until Ronan is on his own."

"Callie!" Ronan put his hands on my shoulders and looked me over with a deep frown. "What happened? Are you okay?"

"Vampires broke into our apartment," Sam told him.

I waved him off. "I'm fine. A few cuts and bruises, but I promise you I'm better than the two vampires who were stupid enough to break into my house. The unfortunate thing is, there were at least half a dozen more raiding the place as we got out." I turned to the housekeeper. "If you have family that lives with you, you need to let them know they have to go somewhere else to wait this out. They're in danger too."

The housekeeper's face blanched, and she pulled out her cell phone. "I need to call my daughter," she said as she scurried off.

"What's the status of the house?" I asked Ronan. "Where are we on the checklist?"

We had a pre-lockdown checklist everyone was supposed to follow that included making sure supplies were stocked and the exterior locks changed, just in case.

Ronan put a hand on my back. "Your staff is seeing to it. Trust them to do their jobs, Callie. We need to get those cuts cleaned up before they get infected."

I snorted. "You just don't want me bleeding on your white carpet."

"Maybe." He smiled. "But I also don't want you to die, so humor me, will you? You can use the master bath in my room. That's where the best first aid kit is. It's more extensive than the one I keep in the security room. You'll need the extra gauze."

I glared at him and walked off to take care of myself.

"Callie?"

I paused on the stairs when Ronan called my name. "What?"

"Don't you want to take your bag up to change your clothes?"

I looked down at my nice white blouse and my jeans, both of which were covered with blood and vampire dust. All I could do was cringe. "We sort of had to leave in a hurry without our packed bags. Don't worry. I've got spare clothes in the security room."

As much as I wanted to shower and get cleaned up, I wasn't willing to take that much time. It would take me long enough to bandage and clean all the cuts, especially with the awkward angle some of them would require.

I went into Ronan's bathroom, found the big first aid kit under the sink, and laid out everything I needed. To see everything, I needed to take off my shirt, which wasn't fun. Some of the blood had dried, and it stuck to my open wounds. I gritted my teeth as I pulled the ruined shirt off and set it aside.

The worst cut was on my upper arm, the one Sam had pointed out. I was still trying to dab alcohol on the wound without flinching when there was a knock on the door.

"Callie?" Ronan called. "Can I help?

I thought about telling him no. Things were borderline-awkward between us, and having him come into the bathroom and see me half-undressed was going to add to that. If I sent him away, though, I'd be patching myself up for the better part of the evening, and I still needed to talk to him about what was happening. Bandaging my side with a blistered hand wasn't going so well, either.

I sighed and went to pull open the door. "Just don't make it weird, okay?"

"I promise to be a perfect gentleman."

"Good enough for me." I picked up the alcohol and the cotton balls, handing both to him before presenting my injured arm and pulling my hair out of the way.

He said nothing but got straight to work, focusing on the task at hand, true to his word.

The silence got thick in the small space, thick enough that I broke it with an intentional "Ouch!" as he dabbed the big cut.

"Sorry," he muttered. "This looks deep. Should I call someone to have it looked at?"

"It's fine. I don't need stitches, and that's all they'd do anyway."

Ronan sighed. "I don't like seeing you hurt, yet it keeps happening."

I shrugged my other shoulder. "Part of the job. You attract a lot of trouble, you know?"

"I'm sorry."

He sounded sincerely upset, so I twisted to look at him. "Ronan, this wasn't your fault. You didn't push the vampires and the fae to war with one another. Vaughn did that all by himself."

"I still feel some degree of responsibility for it since it started with me. I should've seen who Vaughn was, and Jax. I feel like an idiot, and here you are, paying for it. You could've been the first casualty of this war." He finished cleaning the cut and gently applied a generous helping of antibiotic ointment before putting a bandage on.

"I've been on the front lines before," I assured him.

"Well, I don't want you there," he snapped quickly.

I gave him a doubtful look and a frown.

He swallowed. "Just…indulge me a little and stay safe for a few days. Let someone else take the next bullet, would you?"

"No promises."

"Figured as much." He lowered his hand after smoothing the bandage. "That's as good as I can get it." He made quick work of the other cuts, putting band-aids on most.

"Thanks." I put my shirt back on, wincing as the movement pulled on some of the wounds.

"I appreciate all you're doing to make the house safe, Callie, but you know it's only a matter of time before Mab shows up and makes me go back to Faerie. She'll insist the winter court is safer, and she won't be wrong. She'll also want my help to plan our strategy." He paused. "I won't be able to bring you with me. I'll have to leave you here on your own."

"I'll be okay," I promised. "Really."

He nodded but didn't seem reassured. "In any case, I'm going to have the housekeeper get the guest room set up for you and Sam. It's been a long day for all of us, and I'm sure you'd like to get some sleep at some point." He put his hand on the door.

"Ronan?"

He looked back at me expectantly.

"Thanks."

"Anytime," he said and left.

I stared at myself in the mirror, one side of my face covered in micro-scratches and small cuts that stung as I ran my fingers over them. Two vampires and I'd almost gotten my ass handed to me. I'd run when more of them showed up, and here I was telling Ronan I'd be fine on my own against a whole army. Who was I trying to convince, myself or him?

CHAPTER THREE

I turned over in the unfamiliar bed for about the thousandth time. At first, I'd blamed my inability to sleep on Sam's snoring. I wasn't used to sharing a bed with anyone, but the king-sized bed in the guest bedroom was plenty big enough for the two of us. I barely would have noticed Sam in bed with me if it were not for their loud and obnoxious snoring. Even that I learned to drown out once they developed a rhythm. I still couldn't sleep, though.

I rolled over again and stared at the glowing numbers on the alarm clock's screen. Three-seventeen in the morning, long past when I should've fallen asleep, especially given how tired I was.

It's this house, I thought. *It's unfamiliar.* I spend almost as much time at Ronan's place as I did my own, but I'd never slept there; well, certainly not in the guestroom. In fact, I didn't think anyone had ever slept in that room, judging by how perfect everything was. I knew he had a housekeeper who prided herself in doing a good job, but there was clean and there was undisturbed. The guest bedroom had looked like a picture in a Better Homes and Gardens magazine—too perfect to have ever been used. It made me wonder why he *had* a guest room, even if I was glad he did.

With a sigh, I sat up and tossed the blanket aside, sliding my feet into the slippers waiting on the floor next to the bed. I didn't own slippers, but Ronan had sent his people out to do a little quick shopping so Sam and I would have the essentials to get through the next twenty-four hours. Apparently, slippers were part of what they considered essential.

I put on the borrowed robe and carefully opened the door, checking to make sure I didn't disturb Sam. They snorted, then turned over and smacked their lips, but they didn't wake up.

The hallway was dark, with deep shadows. I shuffled down it, arms folded, scrutinizing each shadow in search of vampires. I knew it was silly, but I couldn't shake the feeling that they might be anywhere, just waiting for their chance to grab me and finish me off.

At the top of the stairs, I paused. There was a light on in the security room, and I could hear Ryan, the on-duty security guard, shuffling around inside. At this time of night, he was probably listening to an audiobook while sipping coffee to keep himself awake. Ryan was a night owl by nature according to what he'd said in his interview, but everyone got bored and fell asleep on their shift sometimes.

I thought about slipping into the security office to see how he was holding up. Maybe a little boring work conversation was what I needed to make me tired enough to drag myself back to bed. If I went in there and asked for a status update or to check his paperwork, though, it would seem like I didn't trust him, and the last thing we needed right now was security staff thinking I was hovering. They'd all been hired for a reason. These guys were pros, and they'd just get distracted if I went in there to talk to them.

With a sigh, I turned the other way. There was a light on downstairs, but it wasn't in the living room. Maybe someone else was up and looking for conversation. At the very least, maybe I'd find some respite on the television down there.

The stairs creaked under my weight and I cringed. Good thing I wasn't trying to sneak up on anybody. Just the same, I hurried down and stopped at the bottom in search of the light source. It was coming from the music room. Odd, since Ronan was the only one who should be in there, and usually when he was in the music room, he was playing something.

The door was open a crack, and it opened more when I knocked. Ronan was sitting on top of the closed piano, his laptop on his lap and a pen resting against his chin. He looked up when I stepped into the room. "Can't sleep?"

I shook my head. "You got a song stuck in your head or something?"

"What?" He blinked and looked around as if he hadn't realized he'd hopped up to sit on top of a closed piano. "Oh, no. It's just I think better in here for some reason. I'd play, but it's the middle of the night, and I have all this to go through." He gestured to the neat stack of papers next to him.

I stepped into the room and shut the door behind me. "What's all that?"

"A directory of all the winter fae in the area." He absently ran his thumb over the stack. "I'm supposed to be drafting an email to tell them what's happened and that they should report to the safety of the winter court out of an abundance of caution."

"Don't they have families? Jobs? Lives?" I shrugged. "It'll be hard for them to just walk away from that."

"The court will take care of whatever they need with falsified paperwork. It's all lies and scheming. Whoever said the fae don't lie had clearly never met one." He nodded at me. "What's keeping you awake?"

"You mean, besides Sam's snoring?" I wandered over to the piano bench and plopped down with another shrug. "I guess it's the idea of being alone in the face of this. Kind of scary, you know?"

"About that." Ronan spun to face me. "I know I said I was supposed to be working on this mass email, but I got distracted and started wracking my brain in search of a solution for you. Now I think I have one."

"Oh, really?"

"We're sitting in it." He gestured vaguely to the ceiling. "Callie, this house is a fortress. It might be the safest place on Earth. Could be the only place on Earth that will withstand a vampire attack. The innermost section is solid enough that you could drive a tank into it and the important parts would still be standing."

I tilted my head to the side and narrowed my eyes. "What are you saying?"

"I'm saying you and Sam can stay here permanently.

You can take the guest room and turn it into your suite. Sam can stay there for now, too, but once the war is over, it'll be a small matter to put on an addition. That way, if this ever happens again, we won't all feel so trapped."

I pressed my lips together and turned my head away. "There *is* something I needed to talk to you about, but it seems like such a small thing in light of the war going on."

"Callie," Ronan said, setting the laptop aside and scooting closer, "you can tell me anything."

I almost didn't want to tell him about the loft, but what choice did I have? The building was coming down, war or no war, and we had to have somewhere to go before it did. I sighed. "It's the loft. The landlord sold it, and they're going to tear it down. They gave us thirty days to move out, but Sam and I are having trouble finding a place that meets our needs. I'm worried we'll have to split up, and they're worried about how much it'll cost."

He threw his hands up. "All the more reason you two should stay here! No more rent. No more landlords. Think about it. It's the perfect arrangement."

I shook my head. "I don't know. I don't think so, Ronan. I appreciate the offer, but won't it be a little, you know, weird?"

Ronan laughed. "Come on, Callie. It's not 1950. You're not going to be shunned for moving into my house."

"But you're my boss."

He hopped off the piano and slid onto the bench next to me. "After all we've been through together, I'd like to think I'm a little more than that. Your friend, at least. Let me help. There's no reason for the two of you to shell out money at the insane prices they call rent around here. Not when I have a house that's big enough for all of us."

"It's not just that," I said. "I like having somewhere to go when I'm not at work. If I lived here, I'd be at work all the time. I need to be able to get away or I'll go crazy. Remember how much of a workaholic I was before? I need that time off, Ronan. You know how I get when I don't take enough."

He nodded and took my hand. "We'll work something out. For now, please treat my house as if it's yours. As far as I'm concerned, it is. You and Sam are welcome here anytime. My staff is your staff, my things yours. And if you need anything—anything at all—don't hesitate to ask."

I looked down at my hand in his and shook my head again. "You wouldn't be making the offer if Mab wasn't going to call you back to court. All these court politics and rules are so stupid. It's divisive at a time when the last thing the fae need is to present a divided front against the vampires. We should be working together, not leaving some people to fend for themselves."

"I know." He patted my hand.

"And what's her deal, anyway? It's not like I'm a completely useless person or a strain on her resources. I can fight, and Mab knows it. I'd be more useful fighting alongside her armies or working to keep you safe. Instead, I have to sit on my ass and hide like a coward, hoping the vampires don't sniff me out. It's not right, Ronan."

"You're not telling me anything I don't know. I agree with you one hundred percent." He finally let go of my hand and spun his laptop around to close it. "Unfortunately, I can't change the law. There's nothing I can do but offer you the house. You're safer here, Callie. It's not as good as a castle, but it's better than leaving you vulnerable. I…I couldn't live with myself if anything happened to you."

I grabbed his hand and squeezed it. "Nothing's going to happen to me. You know me; I'm a fighter. I'm more worried about you and Sam."

Ronan smiled. "I wouldn't worry about Sam. They're clever, and a fighter in their own way. As for me, I'll be safely behind the walls of the winter palace if Mab has her way. Chances are good I won't even get close enough to a battle to see it, let alone fight."

"You sound like you want to fight."

He shrugged. "No, but I don't want to be treated like I'm fragile either. Mab's ego won't allow her to consider what anyone else wants, though. I guess that's her right as the queen. It doesn't mean I have to be happy about it."

"What about summer?" I asked, shifting on the bench. "Will Mab and Titania work together against the vampires?"

"Who knows?" Ronan shook his head. "I doubt it. Those two don't see eye to eye on anything. You have a better chance of getting cats and dogs to dance underwater than getting those two on the same page."

Based on my limited interactions with both of them, Ronan was probably right. Mab and Titania hated each other with a passion matched only by how crazy they both were. I hoped madness didn't run in the family since Titania was my mother. Still, if Mab didn't want me to fight alongside winter, maybe summer would accept my help. I'd have to be very careful about how I approached the summer queen since the last time we spoke, she'd tried to imprison me and erase my memory because she was afraid of my powers.

"What about my training?" I asked Ronan. We'd been searching for a decent teacher, and I was supposed to start with one next week.

"I'm afraid we'll have to put that on hold for now," Ronan replied with a frown.

That made sense. The only teacher he thought could help me would be sequestered at the winter court. Since Mab didn't want anyone from her court helping me, he couldn't risk sneaking out now, not with the war on. Before, he'd been willing to risk it. He was a powerful fae, after all, and we could always cover up the lessons by saying Ronan needed a refresher course. That wouldn't work if Mab called him back to court, though. It looked like I was about to be on my own against whatever Vaughn threw at me.

I leaned my head on Ronan's shoulder. "Will you think less of me if I say I'm scared? Because I am. Not of the vampires or Mab, but that things are changing. I'm afraid of what the world will be like after. I miss the certainty I had before all this started."

"The world does seem to have gone crazy, doesn't it?" Ronan agreed, putting an arm around me. "Well, it can't last forever, and when it's over, things will be better. You'll see. We've just got to wait out all the bad to get to the good on the other side. If we can do that, we can do anything. And I know you can do whatever you set your mind to, Callie Hart. It's the one thing I *am* certain about. You're going to come through this just fine. We all will."

I smiled, pushed him away, and sat up. "Not if we don't

get some sleep, we won't. Both of us had better get to bed." I stood and slid away from the piano bench before pointing at him. "I mean it, Ronan. I'm speaking as your head of security now. I need you sharp."

"Yes, ma'am. As soon as I finish this email."

I paused at the door, thinking about telling him to just send it tomorrow, but it wouldn't do me any good to boss Ronan around. He was going to do what he was going to do, and I'd just have to live with it. In the grand scheme of things, that wasn't so bad.

CHAPTER FOUR

The next day, I took the first afternoon shift. To keep people sharp, we ran on staggered six-hour shifts, which meant I worked noon to six, while there was a shift change at three for my partner. By the time I walked into the security room, I was already on my third cup of coffee. I'd slept until nine, giving me about four hours of sleep—not enough to be functional without copious amounts of caffeine. Thankfully, there was a second coffee maker in the security office, one I planned to make extensive use of throughout the day.

There had been no word from Mab, for which I was grateful. I wasn't awake enough to deal with her if she showed up. She could come at any time, though, and I wouldn't be able to ignore her if she arrived during my shift. I'd never considered myself to be religious, but I took the time to utter a prayer that she'd wait until after six o'clock to show up and cause trouble.

In addition to the normal security briefs the staff and I left each other on regular shift changes, I'd added another log. In it, the staff was supposed to write any news of the war they heard. So far, no one had heard anything. I sat in front of the blank log, wondering if I should insert the attack on our loft. Maybe it had been the first battle. How many people had to be fighting to call something a battle? I didn't imagine this war would be fought with giant armies clashing in open fields the way it happened on television. I couldn't see vampires lobbing artillery at Ronan's house, either, which was a good thing. I didn't know how to prepare a mansion to withstand an barrage.

Eventually, I decided that a dozen vampires attacking two people in a downtown Columbus loft ought to be recorded somewhere, even if it wasn't officially a battle. Sam and I had fought two of them off by ourselves, and that was pretty badass if you asked me.

I grabbed a pen and put it to the page, then hesitated. I wasn't a writer. How did you record something like that? I was still wondering when Sam walked in and plopped into the empty seat next to me.

"Mark's out doing a round," I said absently, staring at the page. "He'll be back any minute, and when he comes back, he's going to be too nice to tell you to move, so let me do it for him. Sam, don't sit in the security chairs if you're not on my security team."

"I'll move when he gets here," They propped their chin up, resting their elbows on the little shelf in front of them. "How do you do this all day? Seems boring."

"Only when things go right." I put the pen down and rubbed my forehead.

"What're you working on?"

"We're supposed to record any events that happen that

are related to the war in this log," I explained. "I was thinking of putting in what happened to us at the loft, but I'm drawing a total blank. I have no idea how to start."

"Writing is hard," Sam agreed with a nod. "You can always use the classic beginning line: 'No shit, there I was!'" They made a dramatic gesture with their hands. "'I was standing in the kitchen, getting ready for work. We'd just gotten the bad news that we had to move when suddenly vampires attacked!'"

I laughed and leaned back in the chair, arms crossed. "You should write that. It'd be an instant bestseller."

"You think so?" Sam wrinkled their nose. "Nah, I'm not a writer either. I was thinking maybe I'd paint the scene, though. You were pretty awesome against those vamps. I feel sorry for any that are stupid enough to attack here."

"If any vampires come here, I'll be the least of their worries." I pointed to the security monitors on the wall. "We'll see them coming a mile away. The minute they step through the gate onto the property, the floodlights will come on, notifying us that they're here. Then all anyone has to do is hit the alarm, every security guard in the house goes to their assigned spot, and we kill ourselves some bloodsuckers. We're all staying armed for the duration of this."

"Sounds awesome," Sam said, "except for one little thing. Won't someone report the gunfire?"

"If they do, we just tell the cops they were breaking in and we defended ourselves. There won't be any bodies to deal with, though, if we do our jobs. At that point, we can tell the police it was target practice, and they won't be able to do anything about it." I patted the gun safe. "All these are legally registered and aboveboard. I wouldn't worry about the human police. Worry about the vampires."

"I'm more worried about Mr. Owl." They frowned. "I forgot to grab him. If I hadn't been so exhausted, I don't know how I would have slept last night. Just the thought of what those vampires might be doing to him…"

I didn't think Vaughn's vampire mercenaries would be interested in Sam's stuffed owl, but I didn't tell them that. I understood the sentiment too well. The vampires might still be in our loft, sleeping in our beds, touching our things. Thinking about it made me feel dirty and violated in ways it was hard to put into words.

"I miss having my own stuff too, but we had to get out of there."

"It's daylight now, and we've got a whole staff of people with guns that can back us up. We should go back and get our things out of the loft, Callie. Before they mess everything up."

Sam had a point. With just the two of us, we didn't stand a chance against an apartment full of vampires, but if I took part of the security team with me, we'd be able to clear the place out. It still wasn't safe for us to sleep there, but we'd be able to grab our bags and some of our clothes, making our stay at Ronan's much more comfortable.

I rubbed the back of my head. "I'll have to run it by Ronan. Technically speaking, it's his security team, and it wouldn't be right for me to take them for my own use. Nobody would be covered for insurance purposes if something happened. I've got to think about it."

"But if Ronan approves it…" Sam rolled their hand in the air, urging me to finish the thought.

I sighed. "If Ronan approves, then yes. We can go back to the loft and get our stuff, but I'm not making any promises, especially not without talking to him first."

"Great!" Sam exclaimed and slammed their fist on the house intercom button. "Ronan McCalister, please report to the security room."

"What are you doing?" I slapped Sam's hand away from the button. "That's supposed to be for emergencies only."

"Why? I just saved you thirty minutes of walking around the house looking for him. Now he's going to come here instead."

"Now he's going to think something is wrong and run up here." I slammed the logbook closed and stood.

Sure enough, within thirty seconds, heavy footsteps approached. The door slammed open, and a breathless Ronan rushed in to stare at the monitors. "What's happening? Where are they? Are we under attack?"

I crossed my arms. "No. Sam here thought it would be easier to page you than to spend a few minutes walking down the stairs to find you."

He let out a breath and gripped the back of the chair, lowering his head for a moment to collect himself. "And here I thought it was an emergency. Everything is fine?"

They cringed. "Sorry."

"It's okay," Ronan said, patting them on the back. "Just, next time, maybe let me know it's not an emergency with your announcement? My heart is pounding."

"The war has everyone on edge." I leaned against the gun safe. "But we did want to run something by you. Go ahead, Sam."

"Me?"

I glared at them. "You're the one who made him come all the way up here."

"Oh, okay. Geez." They spun their chair around to have a proper conversation. "Look, we had to rush out of the apartment with nothing but the clothes on our backs. I'd really like to go home and get a few things, but we're going to need backup. I figured we could take some of the guards back to the loft to take out any vampires who might still be hanging around and get what we need to be comfortable here. Callie said we needed to get your approval first, so I paged you."

"Of course, you can go back and get your things," Ronan said. "I'll come with you."

"Ronan, you'll be safer here," I pointed out.

He raised a hand, waving it as if he could dismiss my concerns so easily. "I'm going. First of all, I'm going crazy being cooped up in this house. I know it's only been a day, but I'm not much of a homebody. I'm more used to traveling than staying home, and I'm already desperate to get out. Second, if I don't go with you, I'm going to spend the entire time you're gone pacing and worrying about you. Going puts all that nervous energy to good use. I can watch *your* back for a change."

"And I'm just supposed to let you?" I raised an eyebrow.

Ronan smiled. "No, you're supposed to argue with me, then realize that trying to convince me to act in my own self-interest is a lost cause and let me go. Or we can skip all that for once and get right to it. Your choice. I'm game for anything."

Well, I thought, he's not wrong. That was how it usually went. Was there any point in arguing with someone when you knew you were going to lose? I didn't know which of us was more stubborn, him or me.

I lowered my head, hissing a loud sigh through my nose. "Fine. Let's all go and make a day of it. Why not? Not like there's a war on or anything."

"Perfect!" Ronan said, beaming. "Just let me get my jacket."

After Ronan left, I punched the code into the gun safe to open it, considering the weapons inside. Sam didn't have any experience with guns, but I did pull out a vest and make them put it on. I'd suggest the same to Ronan, but he'd just shrug off any suggestions about his personal safety. The man thought he was invincible. If experience had taught me anything, it was that I wasn't going to convince him otherwise.

CHAPTER FIVE

We arrived at the loft just after four to find the parking lot empty except for a moving truck. The people occupying one of the three-bedroom units on the second floor were just carrying the last of their furniture out to it as we got out. Sam and I didn't know the other tenants all that well, but we waved to them just the same.

The security guard who normally sat in the lobby downstairs wasn't around. Hard to say if that was because of the sale of the building or if he was off doing his rounds. I was leaning toward the former. Once he got the notice that the building was coming down, he would have gone job-hunting. I didn't blame him.

As we went to our floor, the building seemed empty, a shell of the busy, lively place it had been. Those tenants who weren't in the process of moving out walked through the halls with boxes and blank looks, probably as worried as Sam and I were about finding a stable and affordable place to live.

We reached our loft and found the door broken. I

frowned, drew my gun, and pushed it open. The place was a wreck.

The security people I'd brought did a quick sweep of the apartment. They checked my bedroom and Sam's, clearing both. The bathroom door was apparently wedged shut, so they had to go get tools to take it off the hinges. There was no sign of the vampires. They must've just trashed the place and left—typical behavior for a race of bloodsucking juvenile delinquents.

All the dishes had been pulled out of the cabinet, our plates shattered. The pots and pans had been smashed against the floor or the walls until they bent into unnatural shapes. They'd broken our dishwasher, smashed in the front of the stove, and dragged all the food out of the fridge and dumped it on the floor. Thankfully, it hadn't had time to rot.

Books and papers were scattered all over the living room floor, pages ripped out or shredded. Sam found their laptop smashed to pieces and almost cried until I reminded them they had everything backed up in the cloud. The artwork on the walls had been pulled down and ripped apart or otherwise ruined.

Mark and David came back with the tools they needed to remove the door. As soon as they disappeared into the rear of the apartment to remove it, I heard a big crash. Ronan and I looked at each other before I drew my gun and we ran for the bathroom. David had the vampire by the throat, pinned to the wall while Mark worked to restrain his thrashing limbs.

"Hold him," I shouted. "I've got a few questions for him."

"Torture?" The vampire laughed. "I didn't think that was your style, Callie Hart."

"And you think you know me so well." I stepped up to the vampire and looked him in the eyes.

He laughed again. "I do after going through everything you own. I feel like we're pals."

"Well, then you won't mind telling me where I can find our mutual friend Vaughn Meyer." I folded my arms.

The vampire shook his head, straining against the two security guards holding him. "Oh, you just wait. You'll get to see him again, and sooner rather than later. I'm sure he'll want to take his time with you."

I slammed my hand on the vampire's throat. "What are his plans? Where is he attacking next?"

The vampire just spat at me. I turned away and pulled a towel off the rack to clean my face.

"Go on and kill me," spat the vampire. "I'm not going to answer any of your questions. It won't matter if I die. I'm just one soldier of thousands."

"How many thousands?" Ronan asked.

"Wouldn't you like to know?" The vampire cackled as if it were the funniest thing he'd ever heard.

"He's useless to us," I said. "Do you want to do the honors or should I?"

Ronan opened his jacket and held out one of the wooden stakes we'd brought with us. "Ladies first. And it is your loft, after all."

I took the stake in my hand. "Just one more question, vampire. Any last words?"

"Fuck you," he snapped. "All of you! Vaughn is going to

win this war, and when he does, you'll either be dead or in chains!"

I staked the vampire through the chest before he could say anything else. After he turned to dust, I took the time to sweep up his remains and flush them down the toilet where they belonged.

Now that the place was clear, the guards busied themselves in the living room, picking up the books that could be saved and tossing the rest.

Watching them throw away half of what I owned left a sour taste in my mouth. I wanted to get back at the vampires who'd invaded my home and destroyed my things, but I wasn't even sure who they were or if I'd ever see them again.

I didn't know what else to do, so I went straight to the kitchen, wading through the puddle of fluids on the floor to get to the trash bags they'd thrown around. Without a word, I picked up a handful of wet boxes and plastic wrappers, shoving them into the bag. Sam came to help, but I shook my head and told them to get their stuff. I'd clean up.

Ronan grabbed the roll of trash bags and pulled one free. We worked together silently, picking up everything off the kitchen floor and bagging it. My life in garbage bags all over again, just like the dozens of times I'd had to pick up and move to a new foster home. I'd taken everything I owned in black trash bags then too. Some kids were lucky enough to have suitcases, but I wasn't one of them, not until I got old enough to hold down a job and buy one with my own money.

"I'm sorry," Ronan said, tying another bag shut.

I blinked, looking around. All the trash in the kitchen had been picked up. The only thing left to do was mop up the mess. Hopefully, the landlord didn't bill us for the damaged appliances. "Sorry for what?"

"That this happened to you."

"It's not your fault." I grabbed the mop from the corner and started removing the remaining mess. "And before you say I wouldn't be a target if not for you, remember that I chose to be an independent fae. That was why they came after me first, Ronan, not because of you. It doesn't always have to be someone's fault. Sometimes, shitty things just happen. We can't always stop bad things from happening to good people. What matters is that we pick up and move on. That's what's important."

He nodded, grabbed some paper towels from the pantry, and did what he could to help me soak up the various fluids.

"Maybe we should call the police?" I said.

Ronan tossed the last of the paper towels into a trash bag. "What for?"

"To track down who did this. They won't do time for it, but part of me really wants to know who they were so I can punch their faces in."

He turned on the faucet in the sink and washed his hands. "We know Vaughn's behind it. Save it for him."

I spent the next minute imagining punching him repeatedly in the face until his fangs fell out. In my revenge fantasy, I strung his fangs on a chain and wore it as a necklace. That would probably be an even bigger insult than killing him since taking a vampire's fangs was akin to neutering them. He'd never be able to feed from anyone again.

I started mopping the floor with soap and water. "How are we going to explain the dented appliances and the stains on the wall and the floor to the landlords if they come up here? Maybe they won't care about the damage to the building since it's coming down, but I bet they wanted to salvage the appliances for resale." I shook my head. "God, what if they try to make us pay for the damages?"

Ronan put a hand on my back. "For the last time, Callie, don't worry about the money. I'll help you cover whatever you need."

He wasn't supposed to help me with expenses. If I'd been part of the winter court, I could've petitioned for assistance from them, but as an independent fae, I was on my own. Any money Ronan funneled into helping me bail us out of this apartment fiasco would come from Mab indirectly, and she wouldn't approve of that use of her funds. "What will Mab think about that?"

"Who's going to tell her?" He winked and smiled at me, and suddenly I was a lot less worried for some reason. Ronan always knew the right things to say at the right moment. He was good at making me feel better in the face of awful events.

CHAPTER SIX

Mab was waiting for us when we got back to Ronan's house, along with her winter knight. For once, she'd had the decency to wait outside on the porch rather than barge in. Maybe it had something to do with the new security system Ronan had installed. She could have tried to use magic to bypass it, but the alarm would have gone off if no one typed in the code within sixty seconds of opening the front door.

In place of her usual formal attire, Mab had put on a smart pantsuit in midnight blue and styled her hair in fierce angles. She wore dark makeup and carried a large black leather handbag, an accessory I'd never seen her use. She also had a phone with her for the first time. She was on it when we pulled up to the house, but she hung up as we got out. She stood from where she'd taken a seat on the porch, smoothing the wrinkles from her jacket, and came to meet us. The winter knight remained beside the front door, as still as a statue.

"Ah, Mother," Ronan said, walking past her. "I was wondering when I would see you. If you've come to tell me I should report to the winter palace to be safe, you're wasting your time. I have no intention of leaving the house just yet. As you can see, it's perfectly secure. Not even you could get in." He opened the door with a key, stepped inside, and deactivated the alarm as the rest of us filed into the foyer. Well, all of us save the winter knight, who had apparently decided to stay out front and keep watch.

"I could've broken down the door and short-circuited your alarm system if I chose to do so," Mab said. "But I have no reason to go through all that. Vampires, however, won't care about any boundaries you set. They don't share a mother's love for her son."

"A mother's love." Ronan scoffed.

I expected him to keep going, griping and complaining to her as he normally did, but he left it at that.

"What's all this?" Mab asked, gesturing to the suitcases Sam and I had brought in with us. "Moving in?"

"Temporarily," I said.

Sam added, "Our apartment was attacked."

Mab pressed her lips together and shot a stern glare at Ronan.

He raised his hands defensively. "I know, I know. They're not members of the court. I promise I'm not using any court resources. Callie is here because I need around-the-clock security for the time being, and Sam is a security risk if left on their own. Imagine if the vampires captured Sam and tortured them for information. It's better for everyone if they're both here where they can be useful."

"You wouldn't need to have your head of security move in with you if you came back to the palace." Mab chased after Ronan as he went deeper into the house.

I looked at Sam.

"Go," Sam said and held their hand out for me to deposit the suitcase. "I'll get these upstairs."

"You're the best." I gave Sam my suitcase and hurried after Ronan, finding him and Mab in the kitchen.

Ronan was busy pouring himself a drink while Mab continued to try to convince him that he would be safer behind her walls. He interrupted her in mid-sentence. "Are you planning to order me to come back?"

Mab forced her tense shoulders to relax. "Do I have to?"

"You don't have to do anything." Ronan drained the glass and poured himself another drink. "I'm perfectly safe here and far more comfortable here. If I pack up and head for Faerie, it'll look like I'm running, especially after our confrontation with a vampire tonight at the loft. I'd much rather not look like I'm retreating."

"You are not in retreat," Mab asserted. She took the bottle away from her son and got down a glass to pour herself a drink as well. "Not yet, anyway. There haven't been any major battles yet, but word has reached us of skirmishes on almost every border."

"They're probing for a weak spot in your defenses," I mused.

Mab frowned. "And they'll find one before long. I've done everything I can to bolster our defenses, but it's more difficult for us to make more fae than it is for them to make more vampires. They can double their numbers practically overnight and overwhelm my army with hardly a thought."

I put my hands on the counter and leaned in. "Not if you combine your forces with Titania's. Working together is the only way you'll stand a chance. Vaughn is smart, he's calculating, and he's been planning this for a long time. He's not going to screw up. If you want to win, your only chance is to match him blow for blow."

"Don't you think I've considered that?" Mab swirled the dark-brown liquid in her glass, frowning at it. "Believe it or not, I was willing to set aside the bad blood between winter and summer not so very long ago. After what happened in Paris, and then with you, Callie Hart, what little progress we'd made vanished. Our relationship with summer has soured once again, to the point where I can't even hold a dialogue with Titania. All we do is argue. Imagine trying to defend our land when we can't even agree on how to arrange our supply lines." She shook her head. "It cannot be done."

"Then you're going to lose," I said.

Anger flashed in Mab's eyes. "You underestimate us."

"And you underestimate the vampires."

"Enough, you two." Ronan leaned between us. "Arguing isn't getting us anywhere. Mother, I appreciate your concern, but I've invested a considerable amount in upgrading the security here. I have the very best security money can buy, money that you've invested, and it's all for nothing if we don't at least try to stick it out here. I won't run just because there might be an attack. I'm happy to help with the war effort however I can, but you and I both know that as soon as I return to the winter palace, you're going to put me under guard and not let me do anything. I'm of no use to you there. At least here, I can have an ear to the ground. I can monitor the situation and report any changes, which I have done and will continue to do."

Mab sighed, put her drink down, and reached out to cup her son's cheek. "Of course you will. I know you want to help, Ronan. I'm just worried about you is all. At least let me leave my knight with you for added protection."

Ronan pulled away from her. "I don't need him. I have Callie."

The queen wrinkled her nose. "You're joking. Your head of security is no match for my knight. As the winter queen, it is my responsibility to ensure your safety. No offense to Callie, but I can't leave you in the care of an unaligned fae. It would be a bad move politically, as well as strategically. You need someone from your own court here to help if something goes wrong, and my knight is the best fighter in the kingdom."

"His job is to protect you." Ronan rubbed his face. "If he's here with me, who will make sure no one kills you?"

Mab offered a wicked smile and a chilling laugh in response. "I am not a helpless waif, my child. I am Mab, the winter queen, and I did not get to where I am without a fight. I promise you anyone who forgets that will be reminded by my hand. I can spare my knight for a week, Ronan. A week and no more. After that, we will have to have this discussion again. That is the compromise I am willing to accept. Both of us get what we want, even if neither is happy about it."

Ronan sighed and glanced at me. "What do you think, Callie?"

I shrugged. "You know he gives me the creeps, but for once, I agree with her."

"Then it's settled. The winter knight will stay with us. What's one more person in an already crowded house?" He mumbled the last line before draining his glass again.

CHAPTER SEVEN

The winter knight stayed where Mab had left him: standing guard outside the front door. Sam went out to offer him some water, but he didn't respond, so they left it on the porch by his feet. As far as I could tell through the window, he hadn't moved. I was starting to wonder if Mab had tricked us and sent a statue to stand guard.

He turned his head to look at me. I dropped the curtain and took a step back, holding my breath. There was something about the intensity of his gaze that made me uncomfortable, even though I couldn't see his eyes behind that weird mask.

Something crunched in my ear and I jumped. I turned around to find Sam standing behind me with a bowl of cereal. "Sam! You scared the hell out of me!"

They crunched their cereal a few more times and swallowed. "Sorry. Is he still out there?" They pointed their spoon at the front door, indicating the winter knight.

I nodded. "Yep, and he's barely moved."

"Do you think we should go out there and tell him to come in?"

"Sure, if you want to."

"Me?" Sam squeaked. "No way. You're the head of security, you do it. I'm just a civilian with a bowl of cereal."

We both moved closer to the window, Sam peering from the left while I stayed as far as I could from where he was stationed. It was dark outside, and we could barely see him. Heavy clouds had rolled in over the last few hours, blocking out the moon and stars. A flash of lightning in the distance illuminated the gate, the road, and everything between for a second before it faded.

I hugged myself and shivered. "Looks like there's a storm rolling in, and he's standing out there in that heavy metal armor like a giant creepy lightning rod." I sighed and moved from the window to the door. "Better make him come in before he gets himself fried by lightning. That's one story I don't want to have to tell Mab."

I stepped out onto the porch against the crashing of thunder overhead and the sky opened up, pelting the ground with rain. It sounded like God had tossed a billion marbles on a table all at once.

The knight didn't move from where he stood.

"Nice weather we're having, huh?" I said.

He said nothing.

I cleared my throat. "Look, there's a storm coming in, and it's going to last a while. You might as well come inside."

The only sound was the sound of sheets of rain moving across the driveway.

"There's no reason for you to be out here," I said. "Mab

told you to stay and guard Ronan, right? Well, he's inside. You'll be more effective at your job if you're closer to him, so wouldn't it make more sense to come inside instead of standing out here like a stubborn idiot?"

Metal scraped against metal as he turned his head, regarding me from behind the mask. I stared at him for a long moment, studying the strangely detailed design on his eyeless mask. How the hell could he see anything through that? Maybe there was a spell on the mask that let him perceive movement. With its weird design, it looked like a cursed mask. No sane person would put it on willingly, but then again, the guy *did* work for Mab.

Who are you? I wondered. *Why do you wear that thing? Is it because you don't want to be recognized or because Mab doesn't want you recognized?* The only reason to wear a mask, after all, was to hide your identity. Who was the winter knight hiding from?

"Fine," I said suddenly. "You want to stay out here and rust inside that tin can you're wearing, be my guest. Just don't come crying to me if you get struck by lightning or something." I jerked open the front door and practically ran back inside, where it felt safe.

"How'd it go?" Sam spooned another bite of cereal into their mouth.

I latched the front door and paused, debating locking it. I should lock all the doors and arm the system before I turned in for the night, right? But should I do that if he was out there? I sighed and dropped my hand, leaving the front door unlocked. "I'm still not convinced there's anyone alive inside that suit of armor."

"Why is he like that? I mean, have you ever even heard him talk?"

I shook my head.

"The winter knight is capable of speech," Ronan said, coming into the foyer. "And he is alive as far as I can tell, although I have to admit I don't know much about him."

"Who is he?" I asked. "You must've heard stories."

"Stories and rumors," Ronan said, moving aside the curtain. "I heard he was human once. They say he didn't choose to be Mab's knight, that she controls him with some sort of compulsion spell. No one but Mab has seen who's under the mask in all the years he's served. Some people believe he doesn't have a face. That it's been removed, and all that's left is the cold, unfeeling metal of the mask. Others say there's no one inside the armor. That Mab animated a suit and it's some sort of golem."

"What do you believe?" I asked.

Ronan let go of the curtains and turned to me. "There's someone in there, that much is for certain. He has too many small tics of personality for there not to be a real person inside the armor. As for who it is, I couldn't begin to guess. My mother is capable of such a spell, although it would have to be an extreme situation for her to use that sort of magic. It's considered taboo to force sentient beings to act against their will. Considering how long he's been in service to her, he would have had to do something awful to be treated that way for such a length of time."

I nodded toward the front porch. "How long has he served Mab?"

He shrugged. "As long as I can remember. Imagine growing up with him around, following you everywhere you go. There's a reason I don't like going back to the winter palace, and it's not entirely because I don't get along with my mother."

Sam finished their cereal and upended the bowl into their mouth, slurping down the cereal-flavored milk before asking, "How's he see through the mask?"

"That I couldn't tell you," Ronan said. "I can tell you that he is undefeated in combat, and everyone who's been unlucky enough to cross Mab has met a brutal end at his hands. He has no qualms about killing when ordered to do so."

"So, you think he's under a compulsion spell?" I typed the security code into the system, arming the alarm. Even if I was willing to leave the door unlocked, I wasn't going to leave the alarm off.

"That wouldn't be uncommon. Titania uses one with her knight. It's supposed to be a failsafe measure, something to keep the knights from being tempted to betray their queens. If a queen gives her knight a direct order, he can't disobey, but it would take such an exertion of will to do so that it's highly unlikely."

I crossed my arms and leaned against the wall next to the alarm. "Kai didn't seem like he was compelled."

"Oh, he was," Ronan said, holding his hand out for Sam to give him the empty bowl. "You can bet on it."

That should have made me feel better. "Yeah, but he didn't act at all like the winter knight. I mean, does the guy have a name, or do you just call him 'Knight?'" Sam finally handed him the bowl, but only after Ronan insisted.

"Sir Knight, Winter Knight." Ronan shrugged again and started out of the foyer for the kitchen, bowl in hand. "To be honest, I try to have as little occasion to speak with him as possible. I've always been a little uneasy when he's around."

"Join the club," I mumbled and followed him. With nothing better to do, Sam joined us for a late-night expedition to the kitchen.

The maid had cleaned up after dinner, leaving the kitchen sparkling. The mechanical whirr of the running dishwasher filled the room. Rather than open it and interrupt the cycle, Ronan deposited the bowl in the sink, an act that was sure to get him scolded by the housekeeper. I'd already learned she didn't like cleaning up after other people, especially in the kitchen. It was an odd quirk for a woman whose job was to clean up after other people.

Lightning flashed in the window, revealing the world outside in a snapshot of heavy wind and rain.

"Can you order him to come inside, at least?" I asked, sliding onto one of the stools at the breakfast bar. "He shouldn't be out there in the storm, and I don't like leaving the front door unlocked in case he has to come in and go to the bathroom or something."

Ronan laughed and picked up the kettle, taking it to the sink to fill it with water. "I could try, but I doubt he'd listen to me. Mab must've told him to wait right there, then didn't amend her order. It's almost funny, isn't it? Poor guy's stuck out there in the wind, rain, and snow…whatever nature throws at him. I almost feel sorry for him, but not really. It's hard to feel sorry for someone who barely seems alive. Does that make me a bad person?" He placed the kettle on the stove and turned on the heat.

"I don't think so," Sam said.

"Well, if you can't get him to move, you should call Mab and have her issue a new order over the phone. It's not right to make him stand out there. Honestly, he's a threat to our safety more than a deterrent to the vampires."

Ronan turned his back to the stove. He was about to say something when the lights cut out.

CHAPTER EIGHT

The dishwasher fell silent, and the red glow of the electric burner slowly faded back to black. Thunder rumbled outside and shook the window panes. Lightning flashed, casting long shadows over the kitchen.

"Power outage?" Ronan sounded like he was on edge.

I pulled the flashlight from my belt and clicked it on, running it around the room to make sure we were still alone. "Probably from the storm, but someone should go check the breaker box to see if we overloaded a circuit. Hard to tell with so many people in the house."

"Let me call the power company." Ronan pulled out his cell but frowned at it. "No signal. That's odd. I always have good service in the house."

My cell phone rang. I pulled it out of my pocket, the bright blue of the screen lighting the darkness. At least I still had service. The number wasn't one I recognized, but I answered it anyway. What choice did I have? "Hello?"

"You should know better than anyone, Callie, that safety is an illusion," said the deep voice on the other end.

"Vaughn." I ground my teeth and gestured for everyone to go up the stairs. We weren't safe. Without power, I didn't know how much of the house's defenses were still functional. I was still new at my job, but that was unforgivable. I just hoped it didn't cost us our lives. We needed to get to the security room as soon as possible. "What do you want?"

"You out of the way," the vampire replied. "You've been a thorn in my side since day one. I tried to buy you and reason with you, and when all else failed, I tried to kill you. You just won't die, will you? But even a cat only has so many lives, Callie, and your luck has just run out. Now it won't just be you who pays the price. Innocent blood will be on your hands. I didn't want this, but that's not going to stop me from enjoying every minute of it."

He hung up.

I lowered the phone, then brought it back up to call Mark. He had the duty tonight. However, it would not ring through, and I'd left my walkie-talkie in the security room.

"Is he making a move?" Ronan asked. Neither he nor Sam had moved, of course.

"Maybe." I shook my head. "I don't know. Could be he's just antagonizing me. Vaughn has to be responsible for the power outage and our cell phones not working."

Ronan pressed his lips together in thought. "I think we'd better check the breaker box as our first move."

I had to rally my people, but we'd do that first. We left the kitchen as a group, descending into the basement. I'd only been down there once when I got my initial tour of the house. There wasn't anything of interest except boxes full of holiday decorations, the water heater, and the breaker box. Since the basement wasn't accessible from outside the house, I didn't even include it in the rounds most of the time. There was no good reason to go down there except during a power outage.

My flashlight beam danced in the darkness, catching stray particles of dust. The breaker box was on the far wall. I closed on it while Ronan and Sam waited by the stairs to tell me if the lights came back on after I messed with the switches. I shifted the flashlight so I could hold it in my mouth while I pried open the box. All the switches looked like they were in the on position. Maybe it was a local power outage due to the storm, just like I said. Vaughn had probably just been yanking my chain, trying to throw us off balance and scare us out of the only safe place we had.

I was sure that was it until I moved the flashlight to the top of the box. Normally, a big wire ran from the box up through the floor above, but someone had severed it.

I turned away from the box. "The power's been cut!"

"How?" Ronan uncrossed his arms, suddenly on alert.

That was a good question. The only way someone could've cut the power was if they were already in the house, which meant we had a security breach.

"Upstairs," I said. "To the security room. Now."

Sam nodded. They and Ronan raced up the stairs and out of sight.

I moved to follow, pausing on the bottom stair to run the flashlight along the walls. If the power had been cut from the inside, that meant the vampires had a way in, and they hadn't come through the front door. The beam fell on a loose pile of bricks in the house's foundation tucked into the far corner. I left the stairs to tug on one of the bricks, and it came right out. If all of them had been removed, it would have left just enough room for one skinny vampire to wriggle in, but he would have had to put them back.

That was all the confirmation I needed. The vampires were in the house somewhere, and I had to track them down before they attacked someone.

I raced out of the basement and up the stairs to the kitchen, where I stopped to check all the windows. They were locked and in place. Outside, rain fell in heavy lines, pushed into a slant by the angry wind. The storm seemed to have stalled overhead as furious thunder and lightning banged and flashed. In the brief flashes from the lightning, I couldn't make out much outside beyond a few feet.

I pulled open the back door without disarming the alarm just to check, and there was a small blessing. The warning beep still sounded, meaning the alarm was still active. I shut the door and twisted the deadbolt into place.

"Callie?" Mark asked from behind me. "What's going on?"

I turned away from the back door. "Someone cut the power. That means we have an intruder, Mark. I need you to get everyone up. Search the house from top to bottom. All staff need to report to the core of the house."

"Do you want to activate the panic protocol?"

I should, I thought. That would send the house into lockdown and notify the police and fire departments immediately, summoning both to the house. Normally, that was what I would have done, but Vaughn's comment about innocent blood being on my hands had left me uneasy. I'd thought at first he'd meant Sam or Ronan's staff, but what if he was just waiting for me to call the cops so he could have his people attack them? A massacre like that was sure to make the news and be a media nightmare for the winter court. It would force them to fight the war on a front they weren't anticipating—a legal battle instead of the enemy.

"No," I said. "Not yet. Just make sure everyone is safe and then report back to the security room to initiate a full sweep of the house. I want every room searched in two-man teams."

Mark nodded and left me alone in the kitchen. I pushed away from the back door and started through the house for the front. If there was a vampire in here like I suspected, we were going to need all hands on deck. That meant I needed to alert the winter knight.

He was still standing outside in the thunderstorm, letting the rain pelt him as the wind changed directions. I muttered a string of curses as I pulled on my jacket and stepped out into the storm. "There's an intruder in the house," I shouted.

The winter knight turned, the most movement I'd seen from him all day. He didn't move away from his spot near the front door, though.

"I'm going to do a sweep of the house. You'll let me know if anyone comes through here?"

I didn't expect an answer from him. After all, he had never said a word to me. Ronan might've believed him capable of speech, but I still didn't think he could talk. At least, not to me. Maybe Mab had him under a gag order, along with her compulsion spell.

He gripped the hilt of the big sword at his side and nodded.

I hesitated at the door, wondering if I should push my

luck and see if he'd do a sweep of the outside of the house since he'd decided to stay out in the rain. He turned back into the position he'd been in before, though, staring out toward the gate as if he were waiting for Mab to come back to collect him. I left the winter knight at his post and went back inside, taking the stairs two at a time. He might've creeped me out, but I had to admit I still felt a lot safer with him guarding the front door.

Upstairs, I opened the security room and found sleepy people crowding the tiny room. The housekeeper bustled toward me, and I held up a hand. "Not now. Please hold your complaints and questions for later."

She stayed where she was, even if she wasn't happy about it.

No one spoke to me or got in my way as I went for the gun safe and punched in the code. It popped open. I grabbed an extra flashlight, passing it to the nearest member of my security staff. In silence, I passed out weapons, ammo, and a few of the sharpened stakes we'd been working on to the people who weren't already armed, according to their training.

Once everyone had a weapon, I shut the safe and turned around. "Two-man teams. David, Mark, you take the downstairs. I want each room checked twice. If anything is out of place, even just a little, you call for backup. Understand?"

"Yes, ma'am," came the answer in unison.

I nodded. "The rest of you are upstairs with me. Anyone not on the security teams, stay here until I give the all-clear. No matter what you hear on the other side of that door, you don't open it. Understand?"

A few of the blank, sleepy faces nodded.

Ronan broke out of the crowd to stand in front of me. "Be careful, Callie."

I squeezed his shoulder, assuring him silently that I would be. "All right, everybody. You have your assignments. Maintain radio contact and report back in thirty."

CHAPTER NINE

There were fewer rooms upstairs, but because most of them were bedrooms, it also meant there were more places to hide. The first room I took was the guest room where Sam and I had slept.

My partner was a new hire named Nate. He might've been new to Ronan's security team, but the guy had enough bodyguarding experience to put everyone else to shame. His resume included being event staff at two Presidential parades and guarding a guy who later went on to become the Pope. Nate had a lot of interesting stories about the people he'd guarded, which usually made him great company on rounds. For an operation like this, he was invaluable because I didn't need to tell him what to do.

Inside the door, I turned right while he went left. I moved aside the curtains and pushed back the chair. Nothing looked like it had been disturbed, and there were no signs of a break-in. Nate checked under the bed and behind the headboard, even though no one could fit back there. He knew as well as I did that we were looking for more than just a person. If someone wanted to hurt Ronan or any of us, they could plant explosives or traps anywhere. We had to cover all bases.

The guest room, however, was exactly as it should be. Nate called it clear, which I confirmed by getting on the radio and announcing, "Guest room one is clear. Moving to guest room two."

Guest room two wasn't really a bedroom. It was meant to be, but it had been in various stages of renovations ever since I came to work for Ronan. First, they were redoing the floors, and then they were painting the walls. Then it became the room where everything went into storage. There were boxes of old books and antiques piled three high and four deep in there. I kept telling Ronan he should sell some of that junk or get a storage unit, but it was one of those things he never got around to. Some of the items weren't even his but belonged to various local fae he'd agreed to help out by storing their stuff.

I slid behind a box marked TOYS while Nate went the other way, searching behind someone's old sofa that had been covered with a sheet. *That does it*, I thought. *He's getting a storage unit after this, come hell or high water. Then Sam can have this room.*

I paused and shook my head. What the hell was I thinking? Hadn't I turned Ronan down when he made that offer? Our stay with him was temporary. It had to be. Sam and I needed our own space.

A shadow shifted behind me and I spun, pulling my gun. At first, I thought it was just Nate's shadow, but then I heard him moving around somewhere else in the room. We weren't alone in there. With my gun out in front of me,

I carefully closed on where I thought the source of the shadow was—around a particularly tall stack of plastic bins. Holding my breath, I stepped around the bins and pointed my gun at the corner. I saw nothing but a shaft of dim light coming in through the nearby window.

A set of icy-cold hands lowered around my neck from behind. I twisted, ready to fire the gun, but my attacker knocked it away. It hit the wall with a loud bang and fell to the floor. Claws swiped at my face. I leaned backward, narrowly avoiding having it sliced off.

The vampire moved into the light. He was short and thin like a starving man, his face sunken and his eyes bulging. Fangs protruded from his thin lips. He wore a black turtleneck and black pants with his black shoes, and a knitted black hat hid his hair. The vampire was dressed like a classic cat burglar, blending seamlessly with the shadows. Hunger shone in his eyes, along with a hint of madness.

Boxes all around the room tumbled over and more vampires emerged from the darkness, hissing, spitting, and clawing the air as they moved toward Nate and me. The radio at my hip crackled to life, and David reported multiple vampires on the floor below as well. The transmission cut out before he could give me an exact count.

I lifted a wooden stake from where I'd slid it through a belt loop. Maybe I had only one, but I intended to use it as well as possible. "Come on, assholes. Are we doing this or what?"

Two vampires charged me at once. I jabbed the stake into the closest one's chest and tried to yank it out, but it got stuck. To avoid getting hit by the other one, I ducked, pushing the staked vampire away. That meant letting go of my best weapon, but not my only weapon. As the second vampire tumbled by, still trying to recover from his awkward lunge, I grabbed his ankle and sent a pulse of magic through his body, freezing him solid. The next vampire who rushed me slammed into the frozen one, shattering him into a dozen pieces that turned into big puffs of ash.

Nate came out of nowhere with his stake and jammed it into the third vampire's back. Two more jumped on Nate, scratching and clawing at his torso. Nate threw one of them off with a snarl. That vampire crashed through the window and fell to the ground outside, where I hoped the winter knight would finish him off. Either that or he'd join the fray downstairs. I could hear David and Mark shouting, fighting more vampires, but I pushed the sound to the back of my mind. If I wanted to help them, I first had to deal with the vampires in here.

Nate backed against the wall, slamming a vampire into it. The vamp had latched onto his back and sunk his fangs into Nate's shoulder. I grabbed him by the ears and hauled him off, delivering a punch to the vampire's throat. He gargled, spat blood, and grabbed his neck. One good kick and the vampire staggered back to fall on some glass jutting out of the broken window, which made an effective stake.

That left one more, and I'd have to deal with him without Nate's help since my partner had fallen to the floor. "Keep pressure on the wound," I shouted and picked up the remains of my stake from the pile of ash that was the first vampire. The stake was much smaller, having burned with the vampire, but it still had a sharp edge, so it was still useful.

The vampire hissed at me and pushed over a pile of boxes before rushing for the door. I chased him. He tried to duck into Ronan's room, but I caught him before he could, pulling the door closed on his hand. He howled until I jammed the smaller stake into him at the bottom of his ribcage. The last vampire turned to smoldering ash and the door swung open. I spat on the pile and ran back to Nate.

Nate was sitting up, his hand over the wound. He waved me off. "Go. I'll be fine. There's fighting downstairs."

"Keep pressure on it," I repeated and ran to help the others.

I found them in the music room. Ronan's harp had been smashed, and the piano wasn't faring much better. There were more vampires in the music room than I'd dealt with upstairs—at least twice as many. Two security officers had joined the assigned team, and we'd have a talk about that later since they were supposed to be elsewhere. They were down and out, bleeding from wounds on their arms or necks. I didn't think either of them was dead, but I couldn't afford to stop and make sure, not while there were two more to keep alive, plus the others in the house.

I picked up pieces of wood that had once been part of the shattered harp. They'd do for makeshift stakes. With a shout to announce my arrival, I dove into the fight, staking two vampires in quick succession. Another pair tore into David, while yet another vampire backhanded Mark, sending him spiraling into the wall. His head struck with a thud and he fell motionless to the ground, leaving me alone against five bloodsuckers.

I looked around for anything I could use as a weapon, but all the splintered wood was now on the other side of the room. There was a trombone nearby. When had he gotten that? It didn't matter. A trombone wasn't my first choice of weapon, but it'd do in a pinch. I grabbed it and held it up. The vampires snickered as the slide slowly inched down and slid off, clattering loudly to the floor. I swung the trombone like a bat, missing by a mile. Apparently, that was even funnier since they erupted into outright laughter.

I'm screwed, I thought. Why couldn't Ronan have been learning to play the snare drum or the xylophone or something with mallets instead of the stupid trombone? I still had my magic, but when I reached for it, I only managed to summon an exhausted trickle. That was the problem recently; I could get the magic to respond to my call more often, but it got depleted pretty quickly. I had another few minutes before the power returned to full, and by then, the vampires would have made short work of me.

They snarled and hissed, closing in with swiping claws and taunting laughter. "First we finish her," said one.

I swung the trombone at him, but he ducked with ease.

"Then we drain the others!" Finished another vampire.

"I've never killed a fae prince before." Another vampire licked his lips and flexed his clawed fingers as he came within reach.

I smacked him with the bell of the trombone. The instrument made a satisfying sound as it smashed into his skull, even if the brass dented beyond usefulness after just one hit. The vampire staggered back a step, shook his head, and kept coming.

The door on the far side of the music room suddenly crashed open and the winter knight stepped in. The vampires turned, suddenly on alert. They tried to retreat, but it was no use. With a single swing, the knight decapitated two, their bodies and heads turning quickly to ash. The last three vampires screeched and jumped at him. I clobbered one of them with the twisted remains of the trombone, pushing him to the floor. There were two metal tubes at the end of the instrument where the slide attached, and I jammed them into the wood on either side of the vampire's chin, trapping him in place while I retrieved the slide.

Just for the record, you can stake a vampire with a trombone slide in a pinch. Suddenly, every marching band in the country seemed a lot more threatening.

After dealing with one vampire, I turned to assist the winter knight but found he didn't need any help. He finished off the last vampire with an expert thrust of his sword through the bloodsucker's chest. The vamp snarled and hissed, but in the end, he turned to ash like all the others. The winter knight slashed his sword through the air, cleaning off the last burning shreds of vampire.

"Thanks," I said breathlessly, although I wasn't sure why he'd rushed in to help me. Mab had made it very clear that I was supposed to be on my own now that I was an independent fae. The winter knight was the last person I ever expected to help.

The winter knight grunted in response. It was the closest thing to a conversation we'd ever had.

CHAPTER TEN

After the rest of vampires we knew about had been dealt with, we cleared the house, and I checked on my staff. Miraculously, no one seemed to have life-threatening wounds, but I insisted the four injured security guards be treated. Ronan called in some favors and pulled a few strings to get someone to come out, no questions asked. Everyone but Mark probably just needed wounds cleaned and stitched up. Mark, however, needed to be evaluated for a concussion after being smacked with a wall.

Somehow, I escaped the whole thing with only a few cuts and one or two new bruises. The music room, however, was a different story. Most of the instruments had been destroyed, and the few that weren't probably needed repairs. When Ronan saw the room, his shoulders slumped, and his already dark mood sank further. He walked over to the piano and ran his fingers over the broken wood and the busted keys. The house wouldn't be a home to him without his music.

After making sure everyone was fine and sounding the all-clear, we got to work securing and picking up the place. We sealed off the basement, and everyone who could stand was pushing a broom somewhere or picking up glass. As soon as the day dawned, Ronan was on the phone with an electrician he knew to come out and repair the damage to the breaker box. We'd have to figure out how to keep the vamps from pulling that trick with removing bricks to get in again.

With everyone else cleaning, I had to go back to the security room and log every piece of equipment that had been used, removed, or damaged and make sure the guns I'd issued to the non-security people were checked back in. I counted bullets, cataloged stakes, and made notes about what we'd need to replace to be back at full capacity. When that was done, I went through the security footage to isolate the vampire incidents and mark them in the logbook, noting the location and time.

I also scanned hours of footage, looking for how they'd gotten in. The loose bricks in the basement were only one entry point. The rest, it seemed, had come through an open window in the kitchen or climbed up the side of the house to enter through the window in the second spare room. All it took was for one vampire to get inside, and he was able to move silently through the house to let all his buddies in. I was astounded at how easily they got around all my security. Those windows were alarmed, which meant they'd circumvented the system, even if it seemed to be on. Even with our best efforts in place, they'd managed to get in. Short of putting roaming patrols around the outside of the house, though, I didn't know what I could do differently to stop it from happening again. I was beginning to think Ronan would be safer in winter.

It was nearing noon, and I was just starting to think about getting something to eat when Sam knocked on the security room door. I jumped at the sound and blamed it on the fact that I hadn't slept the previous night. Maybe I ought to consider a nap instead of lunch.

"Hey, Callie," Sam said, stepping in uninvited. Maybe it was the lack of sleep, but I had to fight the urge to tell them to go away. They held up a white cell phone. "Do you know who this belongs to?"

I sighed and rubbed my eyes. "No, not offhand. Did you ask the staff?"

"I asked everyone, but no one knows whose it is." Sam lowered the phone, frowning at the cracked screen. "I was thinking maybe it belonged to one of your vampires."

"Oh, they're my vampires now?"

"You know what I mean."

I did. I was just irritable because I was hungry, tired, and stressed, a bad combination. With another sigh, I spun the chair, putting the security monitors I'd been staring at behind me so I could focus on Sam. I held my hand out. "Let me see it."

Sam handed me the phone.

I turned it over. The battery was getting low, but that was about the only thing I could tell from the lock screen without putting in the password. The glass was cracked, but it wasn't so bad that the phone wasn't functional. Beyond that, I couldn't find anything of note about the phone until I looked at the back. The phone case was cracked too. Carefully, I opened the case and removed the phone. A piece of paper fell out from where it'd been wedged between the phone and the case. On it was a series of random numbers and letters. On a whim, I entered them, and to my surprise, the phone unlocked.

I blinked. "I'm in."

Sam leaned over my shoulder. "Who does it belong to?"

The only way to determine that would be to go through the personal files. I started with the texts, which were limited. All of them went to the same number, which hadn't been added to Contacts. Based on the exchange of numbers and Ronan's address, it was pretty clear that what Sam had uncovered was one of the vampire's phones. Maybe it had more useful information somewhere else.

I checked all the apps installed, thinking maybe they'd give me a backdoor into whatever Vaughn was up to, but no such luck. The phone seemed like a burner and didn't have anything extra installed other than a game that involved lining up fruits to clear the board. When I opened the email, however...

"Bingo," I said.

Most of what was in his inbox was junk mail, but there was something in his trash folder from two days ago with a heading involving plans. I restored the email to the inbox and opened it. Inside, I found an exchange between the vampire—whose name was Leon—and someone else named Ian. They were trying to facilitate Leon's transfer to Ian's unit, which was supposed to move on the summer court. Although the email didn't state when or where, the mention of moving against summer left me with cold chills.

I stood, phone in hand. "Where's Ronan?"

"Downstairs in the music room. He's trying to salvage the piano, I think."

I was out the door and heading for the stairs before Sam finished their sentence. "Ronan!" I called long before I ever reached the music room. "Ronan!"

He rushed out of the music room and met me in the hallway. "What is it? What's wrong?"

I handed him the phone and stood beside him as I pulled up the email for him to see. "This phone belonged to one of the vampires who attacked last night. Sam recovered it, and I was able to crack the password and get in. I found this exchange. Look here. They're clearly talking about launching an attack on the summer court, Ronan. Vaughn is going to make a move and soon. We have to warn them."

Ronan frowned at the phone and rubbed his chin in thought. "I agree that we have to warn the summer court, but it's not like we can just walk in and show them this."

"What? Why not?"

"Because," Ronan said with a sigh, "the tensions between summer and winter are even higher than usual after what I had to do to free you last month. Titania will likely take any intrusion by someone from the opposite court as an act of war, and that will leave both courts even weaker against the vampire threat. That was what I meant when I said getting Mab and Titania to work together was impossible, Callie. They aren't even talking to each other.

Imagine if I walked into the summer court after what happened before. They'd probably take me prisoner."

"And Mab would flip her lid," Sam added, crossing their arms.

Ronan nodded. "So I can't go, not without clearing it through Mab first, which would take time. You, however, might be able to, Callie."

"Me?" I grabbed the phone. "In case you forgot, the last time I went to the summer court, they tried to forcibly seal my powers and erase my memory, Ronan."

"I remember," he said, bobbing his head. "But you're an unaligned fae. No one is going to view your appearance anywhere as a threat since you don't represent a particular court. You can move back and forth freely. Or, well, sort of. I know Mab doesn't like the idea of you coming into her court, but Titania hasn't told you that you weren't welcome, has she?"

I put the phone in my pocket. "Not in so many words. It's just that I don't trust her. She might be my mother, but she's batshit crazy. I'm worried that any trip into summer is one-way. I'll need some way to ensure they don't decide to hold me and do a repeat of last month's song and dance. Even if I'm sure that won't happen, I have no way to get into Faerie without help. I don't have one of those portal rings."

"I'll go with you," Sam volunteered. "If they try anything, they'll get more than they bargained for."

"Maybe Kai would be willing to guarantee your safety," Ronan said. "It is his duty to protect his queen and the realm. If you can convince him there's a credible threat, he'll be obligated to meet with you, and you can present your concerns to Titania. If the summer knight promises you safe passage under those circumstances, no harm will come to you. Just make sure there are no loopholes in the promise, Callie."

I nodded. "I can draft a message to him, I guess." Kai had tried multiple times over the last month to get in contact with me, apologizing profusely for the way things had gone before. I hadn't answered any of his calls, texts, or emails, hoping he'd eventually get the message. He'd probably be ecstatic to get a message from me, and even more pleased that I wanted to meet. Now that I knew the real Kai, he reminded me a lot of a puppy, just happy to get attention. It made me glad I hadn't grown up in Titania's care.

"In the meantime," Ronan said, "I'll have to tell my mother what happened here."

We both understood what that meant. Mab would finally issue the order for Ronan to return to the winter palace, and he would have no choice but to obey.

I clenched my fists. "I hate this."

"I know you do. We all do." Ronan sighed. "Look, I can't put it off since the winter knight is here, and it'll be better if she hears it from me, so I'm going to have to tell her. When I do, it won't be long before I'll have to leave the house in your care. Have you given any thought to my offer from earlier?"

"Offer?" Sam blinked and glanced at Ronan and me. "What offer?"

I cringed. "Ronan wants us to stay here. Permanently."

From the look on their face, I got the distinct feeling Sam was going to shout, "Hell, yeah!"

"I already declined the offer," I added quickly. "I told Ronan we'd need our own space and I had to live somewhere else, somewhere I wouldn't feel like I was working all the time."

"Fair enough," Sam said with a shrug. "But we're staying here through the war, right? I don't know where else we'd go that I'd feel safe."

Even Ronan's house wasn't safe; the attack the night before had proven that much. If you'd asked me about it two days ago, I would have told you no one could get into Ronan's house since he had the best security money could buy. That much was true, but where there was a will, there was a way. Vampires were creative and determined. Vaughn wasn't going to back off just because of a setback. He was going to send more vampires and attack again, especially now that he knew our weaknesses.

And next time, we wouldn't be at full strength, not with half the security team injured and the rest of us shaken and exhausted.

"Maybe Mab is right," I said to Ronan. "I don't know that I can protect you, Ronan."

He put a hand on my shoulder and squeezed. "Don't let last night get to you. If it can happen here, it could happen there, as that email proves." Ronan nodded to the phone in my pocket. "Vaughn probably has agents everywhere. For all we know, he's already infiltrated both courts. Blaming yourself for what he's doing is a waste of your talents, Callie Hart. Who was it who told me just the other day that we can't change what happens, but we can change how we react to it?"

Ronan had me there. Still, his words didn't put me at ease.

I shook my head. "What if they attack again? Those vampires got in so easily. If they come back, we're down three people. All it took was for one of them to get in, Ronan. One slid in through the basement, cut the power, screwed the security system in a way we still don't know, and then opened the windows for the others."

"We'll get the security people out here," he promised. "They have to fix this since their reputation is riding on it, right? And as for the basement, we'll bolt steel over the walls if we have to."

"Yeah, we could do that." I sighed. "I just can't shake what he said to me on the phone—that innocent blood would be on my hands. He's right, Ronan. Three of my people were injured last night, all because I let my guard down."

"They were injured because Vaughn's people attacked, Callie, not because of anything you did." He frowned at me. "When was the last time you had anything to eat or got any rest? Both will make you feel better, and you look like you could use the break."

"Shift change is in an hour," I said, "and there's still some footage from last night I need to go through."

"Rest," Ronan said and spun me around. "Sam, take Callie to your room. Tie her to the bed if you have to, but I don't want to see her up and about for at least four hours."

"You heard the man!" Sam shouted, and they pointed to the stairs. "Get to bed, Callie!"

I thought about fighting with them, but the very idea of falling into bed was so appealing, my feet carried me to the stairs all on their own. Work would have to wait until after I got some rest. "Okay." I yawned and pulled myself onto the first stair. "But just a nap. I'll be back up in an hour."

"Four hours," Ronan yelled after me. "Don't make me come in there, Callie!"

I was sure I had some sort of smartass rebuttal, but I was too tired to mutter it out loud. One hour, maybe two, then I'd be good as new and ready to get back to work.

CHAPTER ELEVEN

I dragged myself up the stairs. While I was exhausted, my mind was racing too much to sleep, so I slipped into the security room to make a few notes. That lasted about twenty minutes before Sam caught me and escorted me to our room, insisting I get some sleep. They even threatened to stand guard outside until I did.

Left with no choice, I went into the guest room and sat on the end of the bed, willing my brain to shut down so I could rest. It didn't listen; all I could think about was what might be happening in the summer court right now. For all I knew, the vampires had made their move already. The fae could be losing the war while I took a nap, and that just didn't seem right. I should be out there fighting and helping, not resting my head on a feather pillow.

I sighed and collapsed on my back, thinking, *You can't pour from an empty cup, Callie. You're no good to anyone if you're too exhausted to fight.* I forced my eyes closed and laid there for a minute before I realized it was too bright to sleep. The light was off, but the sun was coming through the curtains. I rolled my head to the side and frowned. Finally a sunny day, and I was going to sleep through it. Just my luck.

There was nothing to do but get up and pull the curtains closed. Of course, once I did that, it was dark and I couldn't see the corners of the room, so I had to adjust them again to let in just enough light. Once I got the light right, I couldn't get comfortable in the bed. I tossed and turned, flipping from my back to my stomach. Fluffing the pillows did nothing to make them less lumpy. The mattress was too hot, too soft, too itchy. Everything was wrong.

Somewhere deep down, I knew there wasn't anything wrong with the lighting, the bed, or the pillow. It was me; I felt guilty about sleeping when there was still so much to be done. The problem was, I'd done all I could. Any future action depended on responses from other people. I was waiting for Kai to get back to me, Ronan to work something out with his mother, the vampires to attack again, for more information, for workmen and contractors. Waiting was all there was. Sleeping might make the time pass faster, and make the wait easier, but it seemed even that was out of reach.

After an hour of trying, I sat up in bed with a sigh and resolved to find something to do with myself. I'd have to avoid Sam and Ronan since they would be on my case about resting. They just didn't understand. Even though I wanted to, I couldn't sleep. My brain wouldn't let me.

I opened the bedroom door a crack and peered out, hoping Sam hadn't made good on their threat to stand guard. They weren't out there. I breathed a sigh of relief and crept out of the room, closing the door behind me.

The stairway was empty, as was the room below, but I could hear voices in both the kitchen and the music room, so those were off-limits. That left the broom closet and the library, and I didn't feel like hanging out with cobwebs and cleaning supplies.

The library had not been touched by the invading vampires, but that didn't mean it was clean. It was one of the few rooms Ronan didn't like to let his staff into, insisting that the last time he had, they'd messed up his cataloging system. I didn't believe that for a second. There was no way Ronan had a cataloging system, not with all the random piles of books lying around. Some of them had been there long enough to collect dust.

I skimmed the closest pile, which was a collection of books on nature. There were field guides to identifying trees and birds of the area, as well as coffee table books with stunning animal photographs. Not my thing, so I moved onto the next stack. It was all old Victorian fiction, books like *Dracula* and *Frankenstein*. I picked up a dog-eared copy of *A Study in Scarlet* by Arthur Conan Doyle. The cover had plenty of creases, suggesting he'd read it more than once. The same was true of a copy of *Great Expectations* I found. How many copies of that book did he have anyway?

I moved from pile to shelf, perusing the various titles without any goal. All my life, I'd never been much of a reader, so I didn't know what I expected to find worth reading in Ronan's library. Just browsing the titles was more entertainment than I'd had all day, though, so I kept going, sifting through the shelves in search of something that called to me.

It was on the third shelf from the top, tucked into a dusty corner of the library he probably didn't visit much. There were no chairs in this section, no windows letting in the bright sunlight, and no ladders. I had to go get one from another section just to reach the bookshelf. The book caught my eye because of the bright red cover, which stood out among the black and blue books on the shelf. I pulled it down, smiling at the book I'd picked up.

I could've remained in the library to read, but I was worried someone would come by and yell at me for being up when I was supposed to be asleep, so I crept to the front door and slipped out to the porch. It'd always been the one place I could hide where no one would find me. On rare occasions where I wanted to get away from Ronan for a few minutes, that was where I went.

Except this time, I wasn't alone out there. The winter knight had returned to his post and stood out there, brooding darkly and silently behind his mask.

I hesitated at the door, rethinking my decision to read outside, but then thought, Come on, Callie. What's he going to do? He's on your side after all. He proved that last night.

With a sigh, I stepped out into the sun, closing the door behind me. "Nice to have some sun after all the rain, isn't it?"

As expected, he didn't reply.

I sat down on the first step, book in hand, the knight at my back. "Thank you for helping me last night. I know you didn't have to since I'm not a member of your court. Actually, you probably weren't helping me, were you? Ronan is your prince, after all, and if you think about it, you were helping him by helping me. All this fae court politics crap confuses me. It must be nice to be you and not have to worry about it."

I twisted to look at him over my shoulder. He hadn't moved.

"I guess in some ways, you do have to worry about it, don't you?" I said. "You still have to do whatever Mab tells you, whether you want to or not. That must be hard, especially if you can't talk." I frowned. "Maybe you can, and it's one of those vow-of-silence things. Are you a monk? Blink twice if you need help."

I snickered at my joke before turning around again. "One thing I can't figure out is how you see through that creepy mask you're wearing. What do you look like under there, I wonder? Probably intimidating as hell. I bet the fae kids tell stories about you, imagining you with red eyes and sharp teeth and so on, right?"

He shifted his weight slightly, a move I wouldn't have noticed if not for all the armor.

"Figured as much. Guy like you, it's no wonder. I bet you like it, don't you? I mean, not in a creepy way. I just mean you're probably a big softie underneath all that armor, aren't you? The big scary looking guys always are." I leaned back, resting my palms on the rough surface of the porch. "You know, when I was in the Army, there was this big guy, and I mean big. Not just tall like you. He was just big like a pro wrestler. They had to make his stuff special. Guns looked like toothpicks in his hands. Anyway, we called him Tiny because, you know, ironic. You'd think a guy like that was mean and into weightlifting and whatnot, but you know what he really loved to do? Sew. This guy would get these care packages and do needlepoint, if you can believe it." I sighed and leaned forward, folding my hands in my lap. "Sometimes I wonder what happened to him. Tiny might've been able to crush skulls in his fist, but his heart was never in fighting and killing." I considered the book in my lap before raising it and waving it. "But then some guy wrote 'the supreme art of war is to subdue the enemy without fighting.' Maybe Tiny knew something we didn't. Maybe needlepoint is how we achieve world peace."

The knight tilted his head. I couldn't see his eyes, but if I could, I was sure he'd be giving me a doubtful stare.

I pushed up from where I sat, book in hand. "Have you read it? Sun Tzu's *Art of War*. It's unofficially required reading for anyone who joins the military. You know, before I read it, I thought it would be about fighting techniques. I guess in a way it is, but it's more of a philosophy book. Who would have thought a book written over two thousand years ago would be so relevant today?"

I stood in front of the knight, frowning. "I wish you'd talk to me. You know, you'd be a lot less creepy if you'd just talk." I sighed. "But then, I came out here for peace and quiet. I guess I'm not very good at it. I don't know what to do with myself when I'm not working or worrying. Ronan and Sam think I'm a workaholic, and maybe they're right. It's a coping mechanism. I know that. If I'm busy working, I don't have to think about what might be going wrong, or how messed up the world is. I feel like I'm doing something, even though I'm not, am I? No amount of checking locked doors and windows is going to keep Ronan safe. If someone wants to hurt him, they'll find a way. You know that better than anyone, don't you? I mean, you and I have more in common than most. We've both dedicated our lives to guarding other people, except I chose it. I have no idea if you did."

He was not going to answer. Why was I wasting my time talking to him? I sighed again and sat back down, putting my head in my hands. "How'd I get into this mess anyway? God, my life would be so much easier if I'd just joined the winter court like Mab wanted. But then, I wouldn't be able to contact the summer court about this threat directly, would I? I know I'm in a good position in some ways, but dammit if doing the right thing isn't complicated as hell. Just once, I'd like it to be easy."

My phone dinged, the app I'd used to message Kai earlier. I dug it out in a hurry to read his response, only to wish I hadn't. Kai dismissed my concerns by saying vampires never entered Faerie. **If they did,**" his text continued, **they'd quickly be overrun by our forces. It's a battle they know they can't win, so they won't even try.**

What about the email I found? I texted back.

He answered quickly. **Could be a fake.** Another message followed. **Look, Callie, I know you're worried, but this war will be over quickly, almost as fast as it got started. The courts will still be standing once it is. The only people we're likely to lose are those behaving like spoiled children and refusing to shelter within the courts. People like you and Ronan. Summer is open to accepting you if you'd like to reconsider.**

That was it. I'd had enough of court politics. I let out a frustrated growl and pitched my phone at the side of the house. It bounced off the wall next to the winter knight and landed on the porch with a loud crack that told me I'd broken the screen at the very least. Ronan wasn't going to be happy.

Slowly, the winter knight bent over, picked up my phone, and held it out to me.

I stared at the cracked bit of plastic and computer chips resting in his palm for a moment before quickly grabbing it. "You aren't all that scary underneath, are you?" I asked, turning the phone over. Luckily, the screen was intact, but there was now a crack running up the back of the case. Cases were much easier to replace than phones.

The front door opened, and Ronan stepped out. He turned to the winter knight. "Would you mind going inside for a minute so I can talk to Callie alone?"

The winter knight stayed where he was long enough to make his point, then walked past Ronan into the house, his armor clanking with every step.

"Sun Tzu?" Ronan nodded at the book beside me. "Why am I not surprised?"

"Because you know me." I picked up the book and held it out to him. "I've already read it."

He shook his head. "Keep it. I'm more interested to know if you've gotten any news."

I looked down at the phone tucked in my palm. "Summer isn't taking the threat seriously. They won't listen to me any more than winter does, and it's going to cost them."

"What do you want to do about it?" Ronan asked.

"As an independent fae, it's technically not my problem, is it? At least, it's tempting to say that they made their beds when they alienated me and they should have to live with their choices. I know that's not how it works. If the courts fall, they'll come for everyone else next. We have to make sure that doesn't happen, and the best way is to go there. Based on the email, we can guess when and where the vampires are going to attack." I pressed the copy of *The Art of War* into Ronan's chest. "Since winter and summer aren't going to do anything to defend themselves against the attack they know is coming, it falls to us."

"Which means?"

I pulled open the front door and smiled at Ronan. "We're going to have to save them from themselves."

CHAPTER TWELVE

Since there was no way to get into summer directly, we had no choice but to go to speak to Mab. Ronan would need her permission to enter summer without it being an inter-court incident, and I couldn't go without Ronan opening the portal. Not only that, but I was unwilling to go into summer by myself. Sam had offered to come along, and I appreciated the offer, but their presence wouldn't have the same weight as if I brought Ronan and the winter knight along.

Entering the winter palace wasn't without its risks, however. Mab had threatened to imprison me if I came since I wasn't a member of her court, and she might order Ronan to stay, which would leave the house empty. Nobody wanted vampires breaking back into the house and going through what was left of Ronan's things, so someone had to stay behind. Sam was the most logical choice. They could hold down the fort until we got back.

"How long will you be gone?" they asked.

The four of us were in the kitchen, discussing our plans

at the table over coffee. Well, Ronan, Sam, and I were at the table. The winter knight hovered near the door.

"Not long, I hope." I looked at Ronan.

He confirmed what I'd said with a nod. "We won't over-stay our welcome in winter, but there's no telling how long it will take with summer, especially if we plan on staying to help with the fighting."

"Do we?" I asked.

Ronan shrugged. "I don't think it'll be enough to just show up and warn them in person. You said they weren't taking the threat seriously. The vampires are going to attack. It's just a matter of time, and if summer's defenses aren't ready…"

"So, you're going off to fight." Sam turned their coffee mug around in their hands. "And leaving me behind?"

"No offense, Sam, but you don't have any training," I said. "I know you want to."

Their head shot up. "Are you kidding? I just did my nails. There's no way I'd risk breaking one. Do you know how much that hurts?" They flashed bright-pink nails at Ronan and me.

I blinked. "Wow, that happened fast. What happened to all the waxing and waning? Yesterday it was muscle shirts and motorbikes, Sam. Today it's painted nails and silk kimonos?" I gestured to their outfit. I figured they'd put it on just because of the slight chill in the house from the broken windows upstairs. Usually, Sam didn't swing back and forth so violently between their masculine and feminine sides. It was more of a gradual shift.

"Yeah, I don't know. Maybe it's stress." They rubbed their temples. "The loft, the vampires, and then the attack last night… I just found painting my nails and getting all dressed up like a dramatic horror-movie heroine relaxing."

"Well, at least you'll have the big empty house to go with it while we're gone." Ronan stood. "Don't go holding any seances in the parlor, Sam. I don't want to deal with ghosts."

Sam's eyes widened. "Are ghosts real?"

"Of course not," I said but glanced at Ronan just in case he wanted to contradict me. He didn't.

Sam stood, and we exchanged hugs. "Take care of yourself, and make sure you come back safe and sound," they said.

"Make sure to keep everything locked down like I showed you. You know when the contractors will be here." I stepped back, hating to let them go.

I might've played down that we were likely heading into a battle that might not go our way, but I felt the weight of it pressing in. There was a very real possibility Ronan or I might not come back. This could be the last time I saw Sam. While I didn't want to think about that, the one thing I'd learned from my time in the service was that it was important to say goodbye. I didn't want there to be anything left unsaid between us, but when I searched for what I thought I needed to say, I came up empty. Sam and I had always been honest and open with each other. There were no secrets between us, and they knew I loved them like a sibling.

Sam forced a smile and patted my arm. "Go do what you do best, Callie."

It was dark outside, but the sky was clear, with no sign of clouds. The moon was full and shone brightly on the forest, making it easy for us to pick our way through the trees and sprouting bushes.

"Are you sure about this?" Ronan asked me after we'd walked a fair distance from the house. "It's not too late to change your mind, you know. This isn't your fight."

I clenched a fist. "It is my fight. I'm half-fae. Besides, Vaughn made this personal when he threatened me. It's as much my fight as anyone's because of that alone."

He nodded in agreement.

We stopped in the big clearing. Crickets chirped in the tall grass, and the distant sound of rushing water nearly drowned out the occasional car passing by on the other side of the river. Ronan slipped on his ring and summoned the portal. I moved to go through first, but the winter knight almost knocked me over in his rush to enter.

I sighed. Some things never changed. He was always going to be brooding and rude, no matter what.

I went through the portal after the knight, and Ronan followed.

We arrived outside an icy palace wall, next to a big wooden door with two guards in front of it. They stood to attention as soon as they saw the winter knight. He grunted as if in approval and pushed open the doors, pausing on the other side to gesture for us to come in. It was the closest he'd ever come to conversation. Ronan and I exchanged glances, then followed him through the door.

The winter knight escorted us through hallways made of ice with ice sculptures. Paintings hung on the walls, hanging from nails made of more ice. I shivered, wishing I'd remembered to put on something warmer, although even with my jacket on, I would have taken a chill in the winter palace. No matter what I did, I was always cold there. For their parts, Ronan and the winter knight never seemed to notice the cold. Maybe being part of the winter court made them immune somehow. All I wanted was a heated blanket and a cup of cocoa.

We came to the throne room door, which the winter knight pushed open. Inside, a crimson carpet ran through the center of the room, and huge evergreen trees stood on either side of the throne, decorated in bright colors. Those were new.

Mab sat on her throne, wearing a sleek silver dress that left her shoulders bare. Her crown was made of holly leaves and berries. I felt as if I'd walked in on a Christmas celebration, although it was closer to the fourth of July.

The winter knight went to his queen and knelt.

She gestured for him to rise. "Arise, Knight. It is good to see you've returned unharmed, and you've brought my wayward son along with you." She stood, smoothing her hands over the shining fabric of her dress. Her heels clicked on the floor as she stepped away from the throne. "Callie Hart, I believe I made myself very clear what would happen to you the last time we met. As an independent fae during a time of war, you are not welcome in my court."

"I promise I won't overstay my welcome," I said.

Ronan stepped forward. "She's here because she has news of the war. News you should hear, Mother."

"News that should have been sent through the proper channels," Mab responded without looking at her son. "It brings me no joy to do this, but rules are rules. Seize Callie Hart and take her to the dungeons."

Several guards stepped forward, their hands on their

swords. I expected the winter knight to grab me, but he stayed where he was, then drew his sword. Rather than use it to threaten me, however, he aimed it at the oncoming guards.

My jaw almost hit the floor. The winter knight was protecting me in direct defiance of the queen's order to seize me.

Mab's fingers curled into fists. "Knight, what is the meaning of this? I gave an order, and I expect it to be followed! Take her!"

The other guards inched forward and the winter knight swung at them but missed. I got the feeling he'd done it on purpose. The night before, he'd landed every attack, taking heads two at a time. If he'd wanted to, he could've wrecked those guards, smashing them in their armor the same way Jax and I used to crush beer cans.

"What is the meaning of this?" Mab screeched. "What have you done, Callie?"

"Me?" I looked around. Everyone was staring at me, even Ronan. "I didn't do anything except talk to the guy."

"Enough of this madness." Mab descended the stairs from her throne. "If you won't apprehend her, I will!" She flung a glowing ball of pale-blue magic at me.

The knight might have been willing to disobey a direct order, but he wasn't willing to harm his queen. He made no move to intercept the magic, leaving that up to me. I had no idea what the spell would do if it hit me, but it wouldn't be anything good.

I raised my hands defensively and tried to concentrate on forming my own ball of blue magic the same size and shape as hers. Mine was a bit lumpy and darker in color, but I hoped it would do the trick as I sent it flying through the air.

The magic collided mid-air over our heads in an explosion that knocked everyone back, even the winter knight. I must've blacked out for a second because the next thing I knew, I was sitting up with my arm in front of me. Wind tore through the throne room from where the spells had struck one another, pulling anything and everything toward that spot. It was like standing next to a tornado.

"What have you done?" Mab shouted again above the roar of the wind.

I was about to point out that it wasn't my fault. How was I supposed to know what would happen when our magic hit like that? She was the expert at being fae. I was just a security guard. Before I could get anything out, however, the tunnel of wind sparked, and a gaping portal opened in the center. The sucking of the wind strengthened, and I slid across the floor toward it. I turned over and clawed at the floor to keep from being sucked in, but it was no use. Whatever power had created that portal, it was too strong.

"Ronan!" I shouted as he slid by. He screamed as he was sucked into the portal, and I wasn't far behind.

CHAPTER THIRTEEN

The sudden quiet on the other side of the portal was jarring, as was the transition from the portal's darkness into the light. The room around me was a sterile white, with bright but pleasant lighting at a level just short of what I would have called harsh. A comfortable recliner had been pushed against the wall.

The rest of the scene I recognized immediately. The portal had taken us back in time to the moment Kai and I had been born. Everything was as it had been the first time, except the room seemed bigger and the moment had more detail. I was aware of everything from the red splotches on Titania's face to the wrinkles in the doctor's gloves.

"What the hell is this?" Ronan said. He waved a hand in front of Titania's face.

"She can't see you or hear you," I said. "We've gone back in time to the day I was born. I've been here before. It's how I found out Kai and I were twins."

"So, it's time travel?" Ronan's forehead wrinkled with worry.

"No, don't be ridiculous." Mab's footfalls were muted as she rushed in long strides away from where we stood to try the door. It didn't open when she pulled on it, so she went to the window. "It's more like a mirror. We haven't moved through time so much as been given a glimpse of a scene, one we can view but not interact with. It's like a reflection of what happened. Callie's powers allow her to open such portals, but inside them, reality can be a little distorted."

"Distorted?" I frowned. That was news to me. I'd always thought I was going back in time as an observer who was unable to interfere. "What do you mean?"

Mab turned away from the window, which also wouldn't open, and huffed out a breath. "I mean, some details may be missing. You can't change the past, Callie, but your subconscious controls how much of it you choose to see or to show others. For example, if you didn't want to see the face of your mother, you might find her identity obscured. Try it if you wish."

I picked up a box of tissues from one of the desks. "So, what you're telling me is that if I choose not to remember this box of tissues, it'll disappear."

Mab rolled her eyes. "No. I said distort, not disappear."

I stared at the box of tissues in my hand. What brand was written on the box? What was the design? When I'd first looked down at it, I'd recognized it as a small cube containing tissues, but the details of it seemed invisible. Now that I was concentrating on it, however, I could see there wasn't a brand on the box, but there were purple swirls on a silver background. The more I focused on the details, the sharper they became.

Surprised, I dropped the box of tissues to the floor. "How do you know all this?"

Mab pressed her lips into a thin line and raised her chin. She looked like she wanted to answer, but she said nothing, choosing instead to glance at her knight. He stood silently on the other side of my mother's birthing bed, directly across from my father.

That reminded me I knew his name but nothing else about him. William Hart. Last time I'd been in this memory, I'd barely paid attention to him beyond a quick glance at his features. In his face, I recognized my jaw, my dark eyes, and a little bit of the stern look I had mastered while growing up.

"Knight!" Mab shouted. "Come help me get this door open!" She grabbed the door and slammed her shoulder into it.

"Callie, how do we get out of here?" Ronan asked.

I shook my head. "I don't know. When I get pulled into these, I don't have a lot of control over how it works. When I leave, it's more like someone else pulls me away from the outside."

Ronan swallowed. "But there is no one out there waiting for us except maybe the palace guards, and they wouldn't know how. I don't agree with my mother on much, but on this we do. We need to get out of here, Callie." He turned away and began searching the walls.

While they looked for a way out, I was more interested in figuring out why the portal had brought us here. It seemed there was always a reason for the moment in time I was transported to. Mab had suggested it might have something to do with my subconscious, which made sense.

The last time I had been in this memory, I was thinking about my mother, wondering who she was and why she'd given me up. Finding the answers to those questions hadn't been the best experience of my life, but now I had the information I'd wanted since I was very young.

Yet I hadn't been thinking about my mother or my birth when my spell hit Mab's in the air. Survival had been at the forefront of my mind, but I'd also been wondering about the winter knight. Why had he behaved so strangely? Why had he defied his queen? Better yet, how had he done it if he was under a compulsion spell like everyone seemed to believe he was?

I walked to the far side of the bed and stood beside the man who was my father. For a long moment, I studied his face again, his broad shoulders, and that no-nonsense expression that said he would rather fight my mother's birthing pains than hold her hand. I knew the sort of helplessness he was experiencing. It was easier for me to fight an enemy than support a loved one. Whenever I didn't know what to do with myself, I found work to fill my time. I always needed to feel like I was doing something that made a difference, that made other people safe. I recognized that look in his eyes.

I looked across the bed to where the winter knight stood. With his mask on, I couldn't see his face, which meant I couldn't know who he was. There were things I still recognized about him, however. He was the same height as my father, the same build as my father, and had that same unusual way of standing. Like my father, he had curled his fingers around the closest object and squeezed so tightly his palms were red from the effort.

No, it can't be the same guy, I thought, staring at the masked knight. But the more I looked at him, the more similarities I saw. They were subtle, like the way he held his shoulders and the slight but deliberate movements of his head when he looked from one thing to another. Once I saw those small tics of personality in the knight and in my father, it was impossible to unsee them.

I stepped around the end of the hospital bed, sliding past the doctors and nurses toward the knight. "Remove your mask."

Mab turned away from the door she'd been trying to open. "He'll do no such thing."

I gripped the sheets at the end of the bed, leaning toward the knight. "There's a reason that portal brought us to this moment, isn't there?"

"Don't listen to her," Mab said, stepping behind me. "I order you not to listen!"

"Take off your mask, Knight. Let me see your face."

Despite Mab's protests, the knight slowly reached up to place his hand on the mask. It dislodged from whatever held it in place and fell into his hand, cracking into two pieces.

The face beneath was pale with dark hair and sad brown eyes. It was a familiar visage, matching that of the man on the other side of Titania's birthing bed. My father's face.

"William Hart," I whispered. "The winter knight is William Hart. My father." But that didn't make any sense. If he was my father and Titania's lover, shouldn't he have been part of her court? I spun on Mab, fists clenched tight. "Explain this. Now."

She lowered her eyes as if she were ashamed to look at me. "Not here. Not now."

A bright blue portal flashed into being behind the bed. Every head in the room turned toward it.

"Come," Mab said, moving toward the portal. "We don't know how long the portal will hold, and I for one don't want to be stuck in this moment forever."

William hesitated, but in the end, he followed his queen through the portal.

Ronan put his hand on my shoulder, holding me back a minute. "I'm sure your father had a good reason for wearing that mask and not speaking to you, Callie."

"Did you know?"

He withdrew his hand and shook his head. "No. I had no idea who was under that mask. I'm just as confused about all this as you are. Mab owes you an explanation. Don't let her trick you into walking away without one."

"I have no intention of that," I said and walked through the portal back into the winter court.

CHAPTER FOURTEEN

By the time I came through the portal, Mab was well on her way to her throne. She climbed the stairs with a determined gait, fists clenched at her sides and her back stiff. Her knight, however, hung back, waiting for me near the portal.

"I want an explanation," I said as soon as I found my balance again. "You owe me that much, Mab."

"I don't owe you anything." She turned around and slid onto her throne.

"I do." My father's voice was deep and dark and had the edge of a man used to shouting orders, but it was also hoarse. He hadn't spoken in a while. William looked at the broken mask in his hand. "I couldn't speak to you before. Am I free of the compulsion?" He looked at Mab.

The winter queen shifted in her throne as if she were sitting on a live snake. "Whatever magic held you seems to have weakened. Say what you will. I'll not intervene."

"So it's true then." Ronan took two steps toward his mother's throne. "You forced him to serve against his will."

"With good reason!" Mab shouted.

"Vengeance and jealousy," said William. "Callie, I have been fighting that compulsion spell since the day it was placed on me, fighting to get back to you. You must believe me. I never intended…" His voice trailed off and he turned away.

I wanted to hug him and tell him everything was okay, and that it wasn't his fault I'd had to go through what I endured. How could he help it if he was under a spell, compelled to serve Mab? I wanted to take his hand and lead him away, go out to dinner, and ask him all the questions I'd always planned on asking my parents if I found them. We'd cry, laugh, hug, and then make plans to meet again.

But there was a war on, and we stood under the watchful eye of the winter queen, who was no doubt already scheming ways to get him back under her control. I didn't have the time. Not now, not with the vampire threat looming over the fae courts.

All I could get out was, "What happened?"

William sighed and turned the broken mask over. "I didn't know your mother was fae. We met by chance and hit it off right away. She was charming, beautiful, and smart. I thought she was way out of my league, but somehow, it worked out. When she got pregnant with you and your brother, that's when she told me. I thought everything would fall apart—that she'd have to return to her kingdom and leave me behind. I was only human, after all, and being with your mother would mean leaving behind my whole life. Until I saw you that day, red and screaming and fresh from your mother's womb, I didn't think I could do that.

But after you two were born, it seemed like nothing else mattered but being there for you and your mother. She resolved to stay on Earth until she recovered, but we made plans to return to summer together as soon as she was able."

"You've left out the best part, Sir William," Mab said, standing. "Long before Titania lured you into her bed, she seduced Ronan's father." She gestured at her son. "He abandoned my court to join hers and left me alone to raise our son."

Ronan frowned. "You never told me that."

"You never asked." Mab started away from her throne as if she were going to join us on the floor, but decided better of it and stayed up on the dais, looking down at us. "She took from me someone I loved, someone I held dear, and because of that, my child grew up without a father. I thought it only fitting to return the favor, so I cast a spell over your father, Callie Hart, and forced him into my service. Titania did all she could to free him, even going so far as to march her armies right up to my gate. It wasn't until I demonstrated how complete my compulsion spell was that she turned her soldiers around and marched right back, realizing there was nothing she could do. That begs the question, doesn't it? Why are you free of my magic now, Knight?"

A dark glint shone in William's eyes as he looked up at Mab. "At first, I thought it was something Callie was doing. You've said so yourself, my queen. Her powers are dangerous and unpredictable. No one knows the extent of what she can do."

"You've been around her before," Ronan said. "When we

came here, and then again when I took you to summer to help me free her after Titania took her prisoner."

William nodded. "Yes, but never for so long. I believe it was a mix of my proximity to Callie for an extended period of time and Mab's extended absence. Somehow, that enabled me to break free of the spell."

"What now then, Knight?" Mab crossed her arms. "Do you want vengeance for how you were treated?"

"No." William shook his head. "You might have taken me from my love and my children, but you never treated me poorly."

I stepped in front of William, between him and Mab. "She robbed you of your free will."

"And gave me a higher purpose. Before I became the winter knight, I was just a man. I was ordinary. Yes, I had loved a queen, but that didn't make me anything more than her human lover. I see that now. I would have aged and died while she stayed young and beautiful forever. But by becoming Mab's knight, I have been given a gift afforded to few humans. I am ageless, powerful, and feared." He put a hand on my shoulder. "I don't expect you to understand, Callie. The situation is complicated. While I cannot forgive Mab for what she did, I also can't hate her. There is enough anger and hatred going around as it is, and it won't change the past." He pulled his hand away and glared at Mab. "But I will serve under your compulsion no longer. If I choose to stay, it will be of my own free will. You must agree to that much, and you must also agree to listen to the warning Callie has brought."

The threat against summer; I'd almost forgotten about

it. That was the reason Ronan and I had come to the winter court in the first place.

I glanced at the guards Mab had ordered to grab me not very long ago. They were back at their posts on the edges of the room, standing as still as statues. I wondered if they were all serving under a compulsion spell and shivered.

Mab sighed and retreated to her throne. "Very well. Clearly you believe there is a credible threat, so let's hear it. What do you want, Callie Hart, besides to wreck my court and undermine my authority?"

I looked at William, who nodded encouragingly, then I stepped forward, clearing my throat. "Two nights ago, vampires attacked Ronan's house."

Mab's fingernails dug into the armrests of her throne, but she kept her lips pressed firmly together rather than complain to her son.

"We were able to fend them off with minimal damage to the house and no lives lost," I continued. "However, in the aftermath, we recovered one of the vampire's phones and gained access. In his email, I found an exchange that details plans to attack the summer court."

"I don't see what any of that has to do with me." Mab waved a hand and turned her head away. "Take your problem to them."

"I tried," I said through clenched teeth. "I messaged Kai, and he dismissed it as nothing. He said vampires couldn't even get into Faerie and told me I was being foolish."

"And you are. For once, I agree with the summer knight. No vampire has ever entered Faerie. It's simply not done."

"But they *can* do it," Ronan insisted. "It is possible."

Mab tapped her chin. "I suppose if they forced someone to open a portal, anyone could." She shook her head. "But even if they did, and even if they were planning to attack summer, it's not my problem."

"It is!" I insisted and took another firm step forward. "It's every fae's problem! That's what you're not getting, Mab. If summer falls, who do you think the vampires will come after next?"

The room was silent. Mab squirmed in her throne and refused to look at me because she knew I was right.

"The fae are strongest when they work together," I pushed. "Maybe summer has the forces to repel a vampire attack, and maybe you do. Or maybe neither of you does on your own, and you'll have to work together to stand a chance. I think both you and Titania are underestimating Vaughn. He's smart, he's focused, and he's been planning this for years. Vaughn wouldn't have made the moves he has if he wasn't sure he could win. Tell me, how sure are you that you could repel a full-scale vampire attack if it happened today?"

Mab cleared her throat. "William is in charge of the palace's defenses. What do you say, William? Could we withstand an attack?"

"Maybe," William answered. "But we don't have enough information about the size and shape of Vaughn's forces. He's been very secretive, and our court has been too consumed by infighting to make a good effort. I said months ago that we needed to reinforce the west wall, but that project has not even begun. Perhaps we would withstand a siege for a few weeks, but an extended engagement would deplete our supplies. Overall low morale would destroy us before then."

Mab's confident expression dropped. "What are you saying?"

"He's saying that without help, winter will fall," Ronan told his mother. "And summer likely will too if we don't go to their aid. It's time to put aside differences from damn near thirty years ago and stand together."

Mab opened her mouth but didn't get a word out before the throne room doors squeaked open. A messenger hurried in, bowed, and approached the throne when she waved him up. He whispered something in her ear, and her eyes widened.

"What is it, my queen?" William asked.

She stood, her face blank. Those in the throne room were silent, waiting for her to speak. "I've just received word that vampire forces have entered Faerie and are closing on the summer palace. They will be there before the end of the day tomorrow."

"We have to act, Mab," I said. "Now."

Ronan nodded. "I agree."

"As do I," added William.

We all turned to Mab. She'd been unanimously outvoted, but that didn't matter. She was still the queen, and winter's forces wouldn't mobilize if she didn't give the order, no matter how wrong she was.

ome on, Mab, I thought. *Be reasonable for once in your life. See this for what it is. The vampires are taking advantage of how divided the fae are.*

Mab turned to the messenger. "The soldier sent by summer to deliver this message, is he still here?"

"Yes, my queen." The messenger bowed deeply.

"Well, don't just stand there. Show him in!"

The messenger scurried off to carry out her command. A moment later, the throne room doors opened again, and a young man in padded armor entered. His bright yellow clothes had been splashed by crimson in several places, and he had a healing cut on the side of his face. He approached the throne and knelt on one knee.

"My messenger tells me you've come from summer," Mab said. "Tell me truthfully what's happening there. How bad is it?"

"There was a small skirmish at the border," said the messenger without lifting his head. "I left as soon as I was bid to do so, and as such, I am unable to relay the outcome of that battle."

"But there are vampires in Faerie, aren't there?" Ronan moved to the bottom step of Mab's dais and crossed his arms.

"Yes," replied the messenger. "Hundreds, if not thousands of them."

"Preposterous!" Mab shouted. "It isn't possible! Vampires can't enter Faerie, not unless there is some traitor."

Finally the summer fae messenger lifted his head. "Our scouts have reported that they captured one of the independent fae and forced them to make portals so they could enter. They're capable of moving back and forth freely now."

"That must be why they wanted you, Callie." Ronan nodded at me. "They came after the independent fae first in hopes of grabbing one who could open a portal for them to bring their forces through.

I threw my head back and laughed. "The joke's on them, then, because I couldn't open a portal if my life depended on it. Don't I need one of those rings? I'd definitely need better control over my powers. Tells you how much Vaughn knows about me."

"We should find the traitor fae and end their life," Mab said simply.

I swallowed, suddenly very glad Vaughn hadn't succeeded in grabbing me. "It's not their fault. For all we know, Vaughn is torturing them, forcing them to open portals."

"Nevertheless," continued the summer soldier, "short of

killing one of our own, one they keep behind their lines under heavy guard, we cannot stop them. Summer has launched two such missions, but both have failed. Summer asks that winter send its soldiers to bolster our numbers. The vampire host is much larger than anticipated, and we need more troops if we are to hold off the attack."

"What more proof do you need?" I gestured to the man kneeling before her. "It's past time to warn them. They're calling for your help, Mab. It's time to be the bigger person and set aside old differences to help those in need."

"I can't," Mab muttered, turning back to stare at the throne. "Titania hasn't apologized, and if I go rushing in to help her, won't she think I'm excusing her past behavior? It's simply unacceptable. But if I do…" She lifted her head and spun back around, eyes wide and sparkling. "What was it you just said, Callie? Say it again?"

I glanced at Ronan, who shrugged. "That you should set aside your differences and help each other?"

"No, not that. The other thing." She snapped her fingers.

"Be the bigger person?"

"Yes, that's it precisely!" Mab sprouted the sort of smile only drunk or crazy people wore. "If I help her, Titania will *owe* me. Why, I'll be able to ask for anything I want as repayment for saving her kingdom—short of summer, that is. It would be rude of me to ask her to abdicate. But if I save summer, the size of the debt owed to my court will be substantial, will it not?"

"Er, that's not what I—"

Mab cut me off. "Shush, dear. Your betters are speaking." She sank onto her throne. "Very well, soldier. You may rise and carry this message back to your queen. Winter has heard her plea for aid and decided that we shall answer. I shall move the bulk of my forces toward the summer palace to aid in their battle against the vampire host, provided we are given safe passage to do so. Our people will fight off this threat together."

"Thank you, Your Majesty." The summer messenger rose and bowed. "Your generosity is unmatched."

Mab waved him off. "Go on, then. Scurry away and tell your queen Mab is coming with her armies to save the day." When the messenger had left the throne room, Mab turned her attention to William and the rest of us. "Sir Knight, I know you want your freedom, but I ask you to stay on and continue to serve me, at least until this crisis has been dealt with. We can renegotiate your position afterward if it pleases you."

William inclined his head. "Yes, Your Majesty. I will take your word and agree to postpone such a conversation until after the vampires are dealt with."

Mab nodded. "In the meantime, see that my troops are outfitted properly and my orders are carried out. We march to summer as soon as possible."

After Mab dismissed us, I followed William to the barracks and found my way into the armory, where I picked through what was left of their gear. It was all old fashioned, medieval plate mail and chainmail. I wondered how either would stand up to vampire claws and teeth.

In the rear of the armory, I found another door that

opened into a smaller room where they kept a limited array of more modern armaments. A Kevlar vest was strapped to a dummy. It wasn't a perfect fit, but it was better than nothing, so I put it on over my shirt. There was also a Kevlar coif, perfect protection against vampire bites to the neck, although it was a little big for me. I appropriated it since it afforded me more protection than a cotton shirt collar. From a dusty chest tucked into a corner, I pulled a pair of black tactical gloves and a helmet that was disturbingly similar to one I'd worn while doing patrols in Iraq. I wondered if that was where they'd gotten it.

While the fae picked out swords, shields, and polearms in the next room, I laid out the guns, which were few and far between. An old AK-47 was probably the best choice for me since it felt familiar, even though I hadn't fired that exact weapon before. Picking it up reminded me of the rifles I'd carried in the Iraqi desert.

There weren't any boots that would fit me, so I had to make do with my tennis shoes, tucking the strings in so they didn't come untied for me to trip on. I found a strip of cloth to secure my hair in a tight bun so it'd fit under the helmet better and laid the gun out on the folding table in front of me. There was still enough time left before we left that I could clean the barrel and make sure the weapon was in good working order.

I was halfway through taking it apart when Ronan poked his head through the door.

"There you are," he said with a sigh. "What are you doing in here? I don't think anyone's been in this room for a decade or more."

"It shows. Half the equipment is worn or badly needs to

be serviced. Good thing I decided to take this gun apart. I've seen playgrounds cleaner than the inside of this thing." I finished disassembling it. Broken down into all of its components, it didn't resemble a gun. It was just a collection of unrelated tubes, springs, and metal parts.

"Callie, you know you don't have to fight. No one expects you to." He came up to the other side of the table, frowning at me as I worked to clean the parts and slowly put them back together.

"Of course I'll fight, Ronan. Considering how long it's been since the last war the fae were involved in, I might be the only person with recent fighting experience. Hell, Vaughn is familiar with modern warfare. These guys will need more than swords and plate mail to fight off modern vampire mercenaries. If we had time, I'd say we should arm all of them with guns and proper body armor."

Ronan chuckled. "Do you know how many of them would be able to use a gun, Callie? Maybe a handful could even hold one. There's too much iron content in most guns."

I paused in cleaning the gun parts to look up at Ronan. "It's never bothered me, at least not enough to keep me from using one."

"That's because you're only half-fae, Callie." He grabbed a dusty, cobwebbed chair from the corner, cleaned it off, and dragged it to the table to sit in it. "You know, there was a time when half-fae were common? The courts liked having them around for exactly that reason. Half-fae are generally more tolerant of iron and can do things we can't. When the world first started to modernize, many fae found it difficult to be among humans and all their machinery.

They found their children who were half-fae or raised on Earth rather than in Faerie were far less susceptible to iron burns and poisoning. You know all those stories from around the time of the industrial revolution where people claimed to have been kidnapped by fae folk?"

"They're true?" I raised an eyebrow.

Ronan smiled. "Sort of. I can tell you that in most cases, nobody was kidnapped against their will, but what sort of person in that day would come back and admit to having spent the last four years in nonstop fae orgies? They'd lock them up and throw away the key. Of course, today, it's a lot different. We don't generally kidnap people, and society has evolved to frown on people having children for those reasons."

"You mean, to strengthen the court's hold and expand their power."

He shrugged. "Pretty much. Besides, when you're basically immortal, your society can only support so many people."

I lowered the piece I'd been cleaning. "How does that work if you don't age?"

"Oh, we do. It's just very, very slow, and being outside of Faerie tends to accelerate the process." He leaned in and put a hand on the side of his mouth as if to tell me a secret. "I swear I really am only twenty-nine."

"I don't have any way to tell if you aren't being truthful." I sighed and went back to work. "Meanwhile, I get all the negatives without any of the perks, don't I? No long life span for me. No court to lean on. I might as well not even be half-fae, except for the magic I don't know anything about and can barely control."

"You'll get there." Ronan put his hand over mine. "It takes years to master even the most basic sorts of magic. You've made more progress over the last few months than I expected. I know it doesn't seem like it, but you're good, Callie. You just need to find the right teachers."

My mind wasn't on getting better at freezing people to death, though. All I could think about was what my father had said, and the point Ronan had just reiterated. While I got old, they'd all stay young. I could work for Ronan for decades, retire, and die of old age, and he'd look exactly the same. William had said Mab gave him a gift, making him her knight. It'd extended her immortality to him, keeping him from aging. True to his word, he didn't look a day older than he had in the memory we'd gone to.

I pulled my hand away from Ronan's and began to reassemble the gun. "Maybe that's why Mab and Titania are both crazy."

"Why?"

"Because they're so old. Imagine everything they've seen, the people they must've known. I bet my father wasn't the first human Titania cared about. Imagine the grief of having to watch as you outlive your children. Imagine burying your grandkids when they died of old age and you're still young and beautiful." I shook my head. "I don't know if I'd want that."

Ronan picked up one of the pieces, turning it over and examining it as he spoke. "I think that's why most fae have withdrawn from the human world. Nobody wants to lose someone they care about. We all pretend we don't get attached to humans, but it's impossible not to live next to them and not care. When I left the court and went to live in Columbus, that was one of her arguments, you know."

"Who?" I looked up.

"Mab. She told me if I left, I might start to age. I told her I was fine with that. Then she described in horrifying detail what it was like to fall in love, then watch the great love of your life decay over eighty long years. I thought she was being a sensationalist."

"And now?" I grabbed the piece from him and finished putting together the gun.

Ronan shrugged. "Now I don't want to lose the people I care about, which was why I came to find you, Callie. I know you feel obligated to fight because you can. I know there's nothing I can say or do to talk you out of it, so I'm not going to try, but we're about to walk into a battle. One or both of us could die tonight or the next night or anytime. I just can't help but think about it. There are things I want to tell you. Things I should say before…" He lowered his folded hands into his lap. "I don't want anything left unsaid."

"I'm not going to die, Ronan," I said. "Have you met me? I'm too stubborn for that. Death could grab me by the hair and drag me off, and I'd find a way to keep kicking."

A hesitant smile sprouted on his lips that didn't touch his eyes. "I know, I know. But let me ask you. Do you still see yourself as just another employee? Let's say that hypothetically I had to let you go for whatever reason. Would you still talk to me?"

I shrugged and stood. "That would depend on how the severance went."

"Callie, I don't want to be just a paycheck to you. I want…"

I turned around, watching him wrestle with what he wanted to say. Just say it, I thought. Get it out in the open, and we can go from there. It wasn't like it was a secret that he wanted to be more than friends. Over the last few months, we'd gotten too close to call what we had a friendship, but it wasn't a working relationship either. There were only two people in the world I trusted, and Ronan was one of them.

The truth was it would hurt if he fired me. A lot. It'd be more than losing a job or an income. Those things could both be replaced. Imagining my life without him in it was impossible, even though we'd only known each other for a few months. Sure, we argued. Who didn't? But when it came down to it, we made a good team. We confided in each other, and he was there for me when I needed him to be, just as I was there for him.

But the job got in the way. It never felt like the right time to take the next step. As long as I worked for him, there would always be a strange power imbalance I just couldn't get past. I knew he felt it too. There wasn't any way to handle it without somebody getting hurt, which neither of us wanted.

I swallowed. "What, Ronan? What do you want?"

"I want—"

A loud horn interrupted whatever he was about to say, blasting twice. I sighed, picked up my helmet, and slid it on. "Those are our marching orders. Time to go."

"Dammit, I haven't even gotten proper armor yet."

Ronan stood and went to the door. "Can we talk again? After all this?"

"I think we should."

He seemed uneasy with my answer but agreed with a nod before going out to hastily find his armor.

CHAPTER SIXTEEN

There was a certain comfort in the certainty of a military march, especially after so many years of civilian life. It was an easy rhythm to fall into, brainless even. My body worked on its own, moving to a soundless beat in my head as I fell in with the rest of Mab's forces somewhere near the front.

It wasn't going to be a long journey. She'd had her people make portals just outside the palace that were big enough for the soldiers to walk through three or four at a time. Much bigger than the portals Ronan made.

Unlike me, Ronan would be traveling with Mab, the winter knight, and the rest of the important people. I'd had the option to go with them if I wanted to, but I declined. I was comfortable marching with the rest of the grunts, and that was where I preferred to stay.

The last time I had made a march like this, it hadn't been far either. Most movement of troops wasn't done by long marches anymore. Everyone piled into jeeps and Hummers and the convoy went snaking through the desert, slipping between sand dunes and down narrow city streets while the locals stared.

On this march, though, there weren't any locals around to see us off. Anyone who wasn't marching had been put to work elsewhere, preparing for the return of the troops or working to establish supplies. Winter was nothing if not efficient when it came time to participate in a war.

We went through the cold, sticky portals and tumbled through into an equally sticky summer night on the other side. It felt like going from Chicago in the dead of winter to Florida in August. The change was shocking enough that several soldiers swayed on their feet as they came through or paused to gasp for breath. The heat hadn't been this oppressive the last time I'd been in summer, but that had been a month ago. Humidity hung in the air as if there were a storm forming nearby. In fact, dark clouds crowded the sky above, hiding the starry sky.

Before us stretched the summer palace, with torches lit along the wall. The big wooden drawbridge creaked as summer's forces lowered it on our approach. In the other direction, the faint glow of another army lit the sky. The vampires had probably camped on the other side of the woods if they'd bothered camping at all. If I were them, I'd launch my attack at night when it would be more difficult for the fae to see. As far as I could tell, vampires could see perfectly in the dark, and a night like this one would give them a real advantage.

Aside from the creaking of the drawbridge and the shouts of orders atop the castle walls, there were no other sounds. No crickets chirped. No owls hooted. Even the footfalls of winter's soldiers seemed muted, given how many of us there were.

As we crested the nearest hill, I got a view of both sides: the summer palace all lit up on one side, and a sea of black movement on the other. The vampires had left their encampment behind and begun their short march to the castle walls, gathering like beetles in the dim woods. It was impossible to count how many there were, but there had to be more vampires than fae, based on what I'd seen the last time I was at the summer palace. How could Kai have thought they'd be able to win the fight without much effort?

Once the drawbridge lowered, winter's forces marched across it. Kai pulled me from the line of soldiers as soon as I came into the courtyard and asked me what I was doing there.

"Fighting," I said, pulling my arm away. "Helping to defend your kingdom. What does it look like?"

"You shouldn't be here," he hissed through his teeth.

"Are you going to imprison me? Hold me in chains so Titania can finish the memory-wipe spell she was trying before?" I shifted my grip on the gun I was carrying.

My brother sighed through his nose. "I think she's got bigger problems at the moment. I just wish you hadn't come. It would have been nice if one of us got through this alive."

I grunted. "If you think I'm letting my brother be killed by some vampire, you've got another think coming. Nobody gets to kill you except me."

Kai laughed at that, despite the obvious unease he felt.

"Fair enough. I won't let our mother imprison you and wipe your memories, then. How are you, by the way?"

We started walking through the crowded courtyard, dodging people rolling barrels and messengers rushing from one wall to the next with orders.

I shrugged. "Oh, you know. Haven't used my powers to destroy the world yet or anything, but I'm working on it."

He gave me a wary glance.

"I'm joking, Kai."

"Uh, right."

He led me under a stone arch into the castle proper. Despite not having any electric lights installed, the narrow hallways were bright. Little glowing balls of what felt like magic hovered in the corners, illuminating the rooms. Long deep-blue cloth runners covered the floors. Unlike the winter palace, the summer palace walls were lined with oil paintings, the occasional nook filled with marble statues of animals like swans or deer. Big windows on the exterior walls would have let in plenty of natural light during the day, but since it was dark out, heavy blue curtains had been drawn over them, giving the hallway a claustrophobic feel. Door after wooden door popped up on the interior wall, but we walked by all of them without stopping.

"Where are we going?" I asked Kai.

"I'm taking you to the war council. Mab said you were essential and that we couldn't make plans without you."

I turned my head to study his face. "How did Titania take that?"

Kai smirked. "She wasn't very happy about how close you two had gotten."

"Was William there with her?"

"Who?" Kai paused, and we stopped to face each other.

He didn't know, I realized. I thought about not telling him. After all, I didn't know Kai that well, although he was my twin brother. Maybe he didn't care about his family history, and my telling him might distract him. That was the last thing he needed on the night before a major battle. But if I were him, I'd want to know.

I pressed my lips together for a moment in thought before asking, "Kai, what do you know about our father?"

"Not much," he replied with a shrug. "Mother never said much about him. I thought it was a painful memory for her by the way she reacted whenever I brought it up. She'd always try to distract me and change the subject. Once, she even got angry at me for asking. After that, I quit."

"But you'd want to know who he was if you got the chance?" I wrung my hands.

Kai shrugged again. "Sure. Why not? I don't think it would change anything. I'm not the sort of person who's focused on my past, Callie. I care more about the future."

"Well, then you ought to know. Earlier, Mab and I had a bit of a fight. We threw magic at each other. When our spells collided, it formed a rift in time that sucked us both in. I saw... I saw our birth, Kai."

He cringed. "Not the scene I would pick."

"I didn't choose it," I snapped. "At least, not consciously. Anyway, while I was in the memory, I realized something, and convinced the winter knight to remove his mask. He's our father, Kai. William Hart."

Kai stared at me for a long moment, then turned away

and started walking again, albeit at a slower pace. "That explains a lot, doesn't it? I mean, I don't understand why he would choose to serve Mab, but I imagine it had something to do with the deep-seated jealousy and hate between the two queens. It also explains why Mother never wanted to talk about it. She must've been so hurt."

"Our father didn't choose to serve Mab," I corrected. "She used a compulsion spell. Somehow, it broke, though, so don't expect him to be like he was before. His and Mab's relationship is a little icy at the moment. Forgive the pun."

Kai laughed. "Well, he'll be more useful to the council if he can think on his own. Can he speak?"

"Of course he can."

"Good, because I'd love the input of a fellow knight on the situation."

We climbed a spiral staircase, going up two floors. Little diamond-shaped windows let me peer into the night, where the army readied for the attack. I paused in front of one of them, frowning. "Tell me honestly, Kai. How do you see this going?"

He stopped two steps up from me, folded his arms behind his back, and turned around with a sigh. "We've already fought one major battle against them in the field. I wouldn't call it a loss, but we were forced into a retreat. That's why we're all in the castle now. I had to pull our forces back to safety, or we would have lost everyone. I won't lie. We had heavy casualties during that first battle. Our forces were decimated. Without reinforcements from winter, we would be screwed, Callie. Summer would have fallen if you hadn't come when you did."

"And then winter would have followed." I turned away

from the window, arms crossed. "Mab didn't want to come, you know. And after the reply you sent me, I was pretty sure you didn't want us to."

"About that." Kai rubbed the back of his head, wincing. "I'm sorry I said that to you, Callie. I shouldn't have been so dismissive. It's just that this has never happened before. Having vampires in Faerie feels impossible since I've never seen it. There aren't many independent fae out there who can open portals. Actually, we thought we knew where all of them were and had them under guard, but we must've missed one."

"Don't beat yourself up," I said, starting up the stairs again. "Vaughn is smart, and he's ruthless. He'd have found a way, no matter what you did."

Kai nodded and walked with me, but he didn't seem convinced.

At the top, we walked into another long hallway decorated much the same as the one below, except this one had fewer rooms off it. We passed only two small doors before Kai stopped in front of a set of heavy wooden doors. They groaned as he pushed them open. Inside was a huge room with a big round table in the center. On it was a map, but not just a flat sheet of paper. No, this map was magic. Someone had conjured a miniature three-dimensional version of the castle and the surrounding land.

Mab, Titania, William, and Ronan stood around the table, with Titania keeping her distance from everyone else. Mab stood between her and William, but Titania couldn't tear her eyes from the winter knight, not even when we entered the room. The tension in there was thick enough to cut with a knife.

"Look who I found," Kai said, gesturing to me. "And she told me some very interesting news. It's good to see your face, Sir Knight. Or should I call you Dad?"

William cleared his throat. "Sir William, if that's comfortable."

Titania's fists closed atop the table, then she lowered her head and hunched her shoulders. "I cannot believe I'm standing in the same room with you, Mab. After what you did, I would be well within my rights to demand reparations."

Mab folded her hands and stood up straighter. "But you won't because I am here to save your kingdom."

"And you won't lord it over her like that," I said, coming to the table. "Don't pretend you're only here for her benefit, Mab. We both know what would happen if summer fell to the vampires. Winter would be next. For you, this is a preemptive strike."

Mab waved a hand and rolled her eyes. "Call it what you like. I don't have to be here."

"I should have your eyes plucked from your head, you vindictive bitch!" Titania growled at Mab.

"Try it, I dare you," Mab shot back.

"I should. Your knight isn't bound to you anymore, is he? I feel it—the weakness of your spell." Titania ground her teeth so loud I could hear it, and I wasn't close to her.

William slammed a powerful fist on the table. "Stop it! Stop fighting! Don't you see where your jealousy and your anger has brought you? Here to this moment, where all could be lost."

"He's right," Ronan said and folded his arms. "If you two got along, we might not be in this mess. We might've seen the vampires coming a mile away and been far more prepared for a situation like this one."

I leaned on the table, palms flat. "It doesn't matter what could've or might've happened. We can discuss that afterward. Right now, we have a couple thousand vampires on the other side of that castle wall. They're going to work together to get over it, come in here, and kill every one of us if they can. Our only focus should be on what we can do to stop that from happening. Whatever bitching and moaning you want to do, save it for after. Right now, let's defend your kingdoms."

Mab and Titania exchanged one last distrustful look before Titania finally pushed away from the table. She swallowed some of her pride, and Mab did the same.

William grunted in approval.

"So," I said, gesturing to the map on the table, "what's the plan?"

"We've reinforced all the weak points in the walls." Titania moved her delicate fingers over the model castle, pointing out places where they'd recently completed work. "The only entry point is the drawbridge, but they'll have to cross the moat to get to it, which leaves them vulnerable. They could also use ladders or some other apparatus to breach the walls."

"What about flying over the walls?"

Everyone stared at me.

I sighed. "Do you know if they have any sort of aerial capability, like planes or flying machines? If they do, they can just fly over and drop people in."

"The portals wouldn't be big enough to move a plane through," Ronan said. "I suppose they could've moved parts through and assembled them on this side, but they haven't been here long enough to do that."

"None of our intelligence suggests they have gliders or flying machines of any sort, but they do have trebuchets." Kai adjusted the model, zooming in on one area near the edge of the forest where several huge wooden trebuchets rolled forward at a snail's pace. "I don't think they'd use them to fling themselves over the wall, but it's not a possibility we can entirely rule out. If they had some way to direct or slow their fall, they could easily land safely behind our walls."

"Then you should position a sizeable force here for close-combat encounters." William pointed out an area behind the walls. "Your archers can man the walls as well as your swordsmen. I can organize that group."

Kai nodded.

"We need to be prepared for the off chance this turns into an extended engagement." Ronan spun the model for a better look and rubbed his chin. "What do the stores look like? How long can summer withstand a siege?"

"We had enough supplies to support our people up to a month," Titania said. "But with the arrival of your troops, things won't go as far."

Mab shook her head. "It won't matter. If this turns into a proper siege, we can open portals here in the courtyard and simply move everyone to winter."

I snapped my fingers. "The portals. That's it."

"What is?" Kai frowned at me.

"We can use them offensively. Zoom this back out, please?" I gestured to the model.

Titania and Kai fiddled with it until it zoomed out, showing the vampire camp and the palace grounds.

"There. Stop." I held up a hand and then pointed at the camp. "When they attack, this will be behind them, right? Why don't we just open a portal and move a small group through it, placing them here? The vampires are already moving forward through the forest, and there's no one in the woods behind their camp to intercept our people, according to this. They can set fire to the vampires' camp, which will destroy their supplies and trap them, so they'll have no choice but to push forward. It'll be 'take the castle or die.' Then we keep moving forces in behind them and pin them between two armies instead of staying on the defensive behind the walls."

William nodded. "I like it. There's only one problem. We'll have to sacrifice some of the inner defenses to make such a move, meaning we'll be spreading our forces thin. Whatever push we make from behind will have to be strong, and we won't be able to afford heavy losses on the walls. If the vampires come over in greater numbers, it won't work."

"Once we push from behind," Kai added, "they'll panic. I think we'll break their line long before they break our walls."

"I agree," William said. "We just have to keep a close eye on everything and open lines of communication."

"It's settled, then." Titania waved a hand, dismissing the map. "We have our plans in place. Knights, spread the news to all the commanding officers, and get your people in place."

Everyone filed toward the door, but Kai put a hand on my shoulder, pulling me back. "No one's thanked you."

"It's okay. I'm not doing it for the recognition," I said and took another step toward the door.

"It's not. If we pull this off, we'll have you to thank. You're the one who made this possible, convincing Mab to come here. Without your intervention…"

I paused and patted Kai on the back. "We're in this together, Kai, even if it doesn't seem like it some days. The only way we're going to win this is working in unison."

He nodded, and we left behind the war room to go win the battle for summer.

CHAPTER SEVENTEEN

Thunder rumbled overhead, and the air was even thicker with the promise of a summer rainstorm. I found my way to the courtyard, where William was separating his soldiers into two groups: those who would come in behind the enemy and burn the encampment, and those who would stand and fight in case the vampires broke through the line.

He stopped in front of me. "Callie, I'd like you to lead the rear expedition."

I was stunned. Here I was, trying to just be a regular grunt and blend into the background, and he was giving me what might be the most important job in the battle. Part of me wanted to argue that there were people better qualified for the job. I'd never led a large group of soldiers on a mission, and the fae who would be following me might gripe at being told what to do by an independent. However, I'd been pushing for days for all the fae to work together regardless of what court they were from, if any.

William was giving me the chance to let my actions speak and lead by example. I was also probably one of the only people there with combat experience, even if mine was limited to fighting non-vampires.

I nodded. "Yes, sir."

"When it's time, Ronan will open a portal for you to lead the troops through. The fire in the distance will be our signal to open another portal and start sending more troops through to flank the enemy. Until then, you and your company will be on your own."

William moved on, continuing to separate people into two groups. I stepped out of line to stand before the small group of fae who would follow me on our covert mission. There were eight of them, which was a good number for a mission like this—just enough to get the job done without being too many to move clandestinely. The people William had chosen were a mix of summer and winter soldiers, but all of them were outfitted with cans of some sort of accelerant and something to start a fire.

"Callie?"

I spun to find Ronan behind me. His hand was clenched to his chest. "What's wrong?"

"Nothing," he said and lowered his hand. "I have something for you." He opened his palm to reveal a small silver band with a simple trio of purple gems, each no bigger than a pinhead.

I stared at the ring he was offering. "What's this?"

"It will let you open portals. I was going to wait for your birthday and give it to you then, but it'll serve you better now. Your hand?"

Hesitantly, I held my hand out.

"You'll feel a little sting when it goes on and when you take it off," he said and slid the ring onto my finger.

I flinched as invisible teeth bit into the meat of my ring finger, warm blood trickling onto the metal and seeming to disappear. "What's happening?" I asked, positioning my hand to see it by the dim light of the nearby fire.

"Fae blood activates the rings' power," he said. "It'd only be a pretty bauble to humans, but you're fae enough that it recognizes your power. It's fitting for you." He cleared his throat and stepped back. "Anyway, it'll help with the battle plans. That way, I'll be able to find you and put the other end of the portal wherever you are."

"Thank you, Ronan." I lowered my hand and fought the urge to twist the ring off my finger. If I tried, I worried that whatever teeth had bit into me would dig in farther. The ring felt alive against my skin. I shuddered, and not just because of the sudden cool wind.

A roar rose from the other side of the wall, followed by the double blast of a horn that echoed through the valley and off the castle walls. The vampires were about to begin their charge.

I readied my gun and looked at William, who nodded at Ronan. Ronan spun his hand in a circle, his movements quickening with each spiral. A bright blue portal opened in front of him, and he stepped back. "Good luck, Callie. Come back in one piece."

A thought occurred to me as I stepped through the portal. This was the part in every movie where the main character gave his troops a rousing speech, telling them to be brave in the face of death or promising them vengeance, victory, or whatever theme was important to the film. I hadn't said a word to the men at my back, yet they followed me through the sticky blue portal all the same.

The ground on the other side was uneven and I slid. It took a moment for me to realize I was standing in mud. Rain was falling where the camp was, making the camp-fires hiss and the ground soften. Canvas tents flapped in the increasing breeze, their lines pulling tight to keep them in the ground.

The eight fae soldiers came through the portal behind me in silence. I gestured for half of them to circle the camp clockwise while I led my people counterclockwise. There were still vampires keeping guard in the camp, but it was a token force, easy enough to overcome if we were quiet and careful.

I spied the first vampire as I stepped around the nearest tent. He stood with his back to us, leaning on a pole. With a simple gesture, I sent one of the fae forward, brandishing a stake. Rather than drive the stake into the vampire's chest, he tugged a knife from his side and crept up behind the vampire. In one swift motion, he cut the vampire's throat deep enough to sever his vocal cords and then staked him, silently reducing him to nothing more than a pile of damp gray dust.

Another vampire came out of one of the tents straight ahead. I raised my gun to fire, but before I could, the fae soldier threw his knife. It caught the vampire in the throat just above his chest. The vampire stumbled backward, pawing desperately at the knife. Another fae moved in to finish the job.

One by one, the vampires fell as we made our way around the camp as quietly as possible.

Two vampires stood guard at the supply tent. My team made short work of them, coming in from either side to kill both at once.

Another scurried around a makeshift kitchen, stirring pots of something that looked like blood with vegetables in it. The smell made my stomach turn. He looked up from his work and hissed at us, but three fae closed in and staked him through the chest without him putting up much of a fight.

Two more vampires were making rounds at the edge of the camp. They suspected something was up when they heard the cook hiss, but by the time they arrived to assist him, it was too late. There was a short fight, but it ended quickly when I shot them in the back and let the others stake what was left.

By the time we finished, the battle at the castle looked to be in full swing. The din of metal striking metal and wood filled the air like a rock concert where only the drummers had shown up. Every once in a while, someone would blow a horn a few times, but there didn't seem to be any rhyme or reason to it that I could make out from the vampire camp. The trebuchets creaked, groaned, and fired with loud *whack-whoosh-thwangs,* followed by distant crashes. I tried not to think of the damage they might be doing to the castle walls and the fae manning them.

Once we were sure the vampire camp was empty, it was time to set the tents alight. I went around with the winter fae, pouring accelerant on as many tents as we could. The summer fae followed us, either lighting fires with matches or hitting them with fireballs. After a few tents, the fire spread on its own, jumping from tent to tent and devouring everything in its path. Soon, the blaze reached high into the darkening sky, painting it with a reddish-orange hue.

More thunder rumbled, and the sky opened up. Fat raindrops fell on the flames, hissing as the fire devoured them along with the canvas and wood. I was worried at first that the rain would put out the fires we'd set, but it didn't fall fast enough. The fire was hungry and continued to leap from wooden posts to ropes and to canvas tent flaps.

"Come on," I shouted. "We need to get clear of the camp!"

The portal would open wherever we were to let the reinforcements through, and I didn't want them coming into a burning camp where they'd breathe in smoke.

My tiny company raced to the edge of the camp, and the ring on my finger buzzed with energy. I lifted my hand in front of my face, and the portal sprang into being just ahead of me. Soldiers poured through it two at a time, forming battle lines on either side. The plan was to march straight forward and take the vampire rear guard by surprise, then punch through their line and squeeze them, widening the gap in the center of their forces. The soldiers had to form a wedge formation. When we had enough men to do that, I ordered them forward.

There was no way to mask the sound of hundreds of fae marching all at once, so they heard us coming. A small group of vampires broke away to engage, but there weren't enough to make a difference. The fae forces cut through the vampires and slammed into the rear line like a battering ram, forcing their way into the battle.

Fighting erupted around me. Instead of one big battle, there were hundreds of one-on-two or one-on-one fights in every direction I turned. I raised my gun and popped off a few rounds, killing what vampires I could, but at a distance, it was impossible to pick out which soldiers were vampires and which were fae.

I was lost in the chaos of the fight somewhere near the middle of the fae formation. I could hear fighting ahead of me and see swords and shields moving, but I couldn't get a shot off without potentially shooting one of my own. It wasn't until we'd punched a much larger hole in the vampire rear guard that I was able to break free of the tight line, shoulder my gun, and fire a few rounds.

Vampires weren't easily killed by bullets, but put enough of them in any target and it will go down. Rather than aiming for the head or the chest, I hit limbs, breaking arms and taking legs off at the knee. Vampires folded or were otherwise pushed back when the bullets hit them, making it easier for the fae to stab them through the heart with their swords, effectively staking them.

We pushed apart the vampire forces, separating them into two groups, exactly as we'd planned. The space directly in front of the drawbridge opened, full of piles of ash and wounded fae scrambling to get out of the way of the fight. One of the trebuchets caught fire and fell over in a burning heap with a loud bang.

I lowered my gun and turned, searching the chaos for

something I could do and trying to catch my breath at the same time. My eyes stopped on a small rise in the distance where a lone vampire stood. I peered through the gun's scope, finding Vaughn's smiling face in my crosshairs.

"Got you, you bastard," I said and pulled the trigger.

I knew the bullet wouldn't kill him, but hitting him square between the eyes would be unmatched satisfaction, so I kept watching through the scope, waiting for him to fall over, stunned by the bullet hitting him in the head.

Instead, Vaughn reached out and caught the bullet with his black-gloved hand. I wouldn't have believed it until I watched him unfold his fingers and hold it up between his index and thumb with a smug, victorious grin on his face.

The vampire horns sounded and the fae around me let out a victory cry, thinking we'd beaten them.

They couldn't have been more wrong.

I shifted the scope to the side, watching as hundreds of new vampires clawed their way over the hill. Where the hell had they come from? The camp was empty. The woods, I thought, lowering the gun. He must've had them positioned there as reinforcements. Why hadn't we seen them on the magic map? The bastard had used the same technique I had, only he'd done us one better. The camp and its guards had been a decoy, drawing us into a false sense of confidence.

"Shit," I muttered and backed toward the drawbridge. "Form up! Get in your lines! They're coming from behind!"

Suddenly, I had chaos on my hands, trying to pull my people away from battles they were committed to and get them back in line to form some sort of viable defense. Our whole plan had been to get the vampires fighting on three fronts, but it'd backfired, and now we were back on the defensive. Not only that, but my men were trapped on this side of the castle with no walls to retreat behind. With vampires on either side and closing from the high ground and nothing but stone and a long drop at our backs, our only choice was to stand and fight to the last.

CHAPTER EIGHTEEN

I got about a third of our small mass of troops back to the center in two lines. The rest had either been injured or had to keep fighting on either side to keep the vampire forces from closing on us. The vampires started down the hill. Rather than let them come to us, I pushed our forces toward them, meeting them farther away from the two new fronts we'd created. That would give us more room to maneuver. It wasn't the best position to be in, however, since if we lost the ground we'd gained on either side, there would be no retreat open.

We clashed with the vampires at the bottom of the hill. Some of them leapt off the ground and threw themselves into the second line. Those who didn't were cut down or slashed relentlessly at the armored soldiers. The vampires didn't wear heavy armor like the fae, which left them to be more easily staked, but there were more of them, outnumbering the fae at least two to one. They were also faster and more agile, which meant it required two or more fae to take one of them down. I put the gun to my shoulder and mowed down a line of vampires, peppering bullets into their shoulders, arms, and faces. As before, it didn't put them down, but it did slow them enough that others could follow behind me and finish them off.

We might have started the fight in straight lines, but those lines quickly folded, then overlapped and disappeared. In no time, there was fighting in front of and behind me. I swung my gun around, pointing it at the closest vampire, who exploded in a cloud of dust before I got off a shot. Two of my people scurried by, one of them screaming and trying to pry a vampire off his neck while the other tried to stake it.

I spun the other way and fired. The bullet grazed the vampire's cheek but didn't slow him down. He charged me, swatted the gun aside, and chomped down on the Kevlar collar I'd put on. With a grunt, I pulled free the knife I'd brought with me and stabbed him three times in the ribs before I found the heart. He exploded into ash that I accidentally breathed in. I doubled over coughing, leaving myself exposed.

Another vampire leapt onto my back, tearing and clawing at my armor, and the extra weight threw me off-balance. I fell face-first into the mud, my mouth and nose buried in an inch of it. Panicking, I tried to pull the vampire off my back, but I couldn't get to him. My only hope was to roll over. I twisted my hips, pivoted my weight, and rolled to the side. The vampire's head smashed against an exposed tree root and he lay there, wide-eyed and stunned. I seized the moment and jammed the knife into his chest.

As soon as I killed him, two more vampires appeared in

front of me. I scrambled to get my gun up in time, but when I pulled the trigger, it clicked—empty. That didn't mean useless. I gripped the gun by the barrel guard and swung it like a bat. It connected with one vampire's head with a loud crack, laying him out in the mud, his head twisted the wrong way. He wasn't dead, but he wouldn't be getting up to fight anytime soon, so I turned my attention to the next vampire. He'd been distracted by another fae who'd gone down, and he sprang at him.

I struggled to my feet. Everywhere I looked, there were vampires—three for every fae it seemed. Almost all the bodies on the ground belonged to my people. Our forces were being decimated. Even if we rallied now, there was no hope of mounting a reasonable defense from the position we were in. There was no choice but to retreat.

"Fall back!" I shouted and took several steps back before turning around.

A vampire rushed me, and I was unarmed. I'd lost my knife somewhere, and the gun had fallen into the mud. Rather than waste my time trying to retrieve either weapon, I threw a punch when the vampire came within range. His head snapped to the side before he slowly turned back to me, hissing. I delivered a kick to his hip, forcing his body to fold. While he was fighting to stay upright, I kicked him again in the side of the knee, and it bent awkwardly with a loud snap. The vampire went down, alive but out of the fight.

The lines on either side had broken, and vampires were flooding the area in front of the drawbridge. Without my gun, I didn't have a useful weapon. I knelt and picked up a sword from one of the fallen fae, using it to cut through any vampires who got in the way. "Fall back!" I shouted again. "Behind the walls!"

The drawbridge groaned. Chains creaked and clinked as it came down. Vampires scrambled to get to the drawbridge while it was down, but they wouldn't take it easily. William and Kai stormed out onto the drawbridge with battle cries and a dozen soldiers each to push them back. They left just enough room for my men and me to break through into safety.

I stumbled into the courtyard, exhausted and aching, but one look back over my shoulder told me this wasn't over. I ran back to assist Kai and William, pushing vampires off the drawbridge so it could close. The drawbridge started up, and I kicked the last vampire off the edge just as it rose off the ground. He flew into the moat. Several more vampires threw themselves at it, trying to catch the drawbridge and scale it before it went up. Archers from the walls picked them off with ease, turning them into desperate puffs of ash that blew away.

The drawbridge shuddered closed with a loud bang and everyone in the courtyard took a deep breath, holding it as we waited to see if the vampires would find some new way over the walls. They didn't. I turned away, scanning the tired faces in the courtyard. How many of the people from my team had made it back? It was impossible to tell. There were too many people crammed into that tiny space, too many faces caked with mud, blood, and who knew what else.

I pushed through the stunned and exhausted soldiers who were standing around, waiting for the next wave, for the next order, for the next anything to happen. I needed to find William or Kai so we could decide what to do next, but I couldn't find them anywhere. They shouldn't have been far. They had been with me just a moment ago on the bridge.

I pushed past wounded fae being carried further into the palace or triaged in place if they were bad off enough. Healers moved through the ragged lines. One of them stopped me to see if I needed anything. For the first time, I looked myself over and determined I was fine other than a few scrapes and bruises that would heal in their own time.

After the healer left me to go see to more serious cases, I looked up and saw someone running toward me. He wore the light armor of an archer, but I didn't know his face. He stopped in front of me, short of breath. "The queen requests your presence, ma'am."

"Which queen?" The question fell out of my mouth before I could stop myself. It didn't matter which queen wanted to see me. I was going either way.

"Both Their Majesties, actually." He straightened, finally able to draw a full, deep breath. "Come, I'm supposed to take you to them."

I looked at the soldiers littering the courtyard, and my eyes paused on a giant boulder that had smashed its way over the castle walls to land on a stone staircase. That section of the walls was no longer accessible, at least not until they got the boulder moved. A handful of men were grunting, working to push it aside to no avail. "I'm needed here. In case something happens."

"It's about Prince Ronan."

My stomach lurched into my chest and then sank like a rock in a pond, an awful feeling that something wasn't right. Suddenly, the boulder didn't seem as important. I turned away from it and followed the messenger into the palace.

He walked at a painfully slow pace. I wanted to run, to sprint at full speed to wherever Ronan and the two queens waited, but I didn't know where that was. All the while, worst-case scenarios ran through my head. I imagined him hurt, dying or dead, lying on the throne room floor or in his mother's lap while she wept and wailed over him. Ronan shouldn't have been anywhere near the battle. He wasn't a fighter, despite his best attempts to prove he was. I knew he'd done something stupid and gotten himself hurt, knew it like I knew we were walking too slowly. When I got to him, if he survived, I was going to give him the lecture of a lifetime about personal safety.

I pushed my pace faster, almost eclipsing the messenger in the hope that he would speed up. He didn't. Just my luck. "How bad is he?"

"I don't know." The messenger shook his head. "I haven't seen him."

We stopped in front of the throne room doors, which stood open. Inside, Kai and William were standing guard. The scene beyond them was eerily similar to the one I'd imagined. Mab knelt in the center of the room, with Titania across from her. Ronan was draped over her lap while a healer in a white bandana put her hands on Ronan's shoulder.

"Ronan!" I shouted and pushed through the two knights. "Please tell me he's not dead."

"No," said Mab, with relief in her voice.

"I'm not that easy to kill." Ronan's voice was strained. He pushed the healer away and struggled to sit up.

"You shouldn't sit up," Mab said, so he did it anyway just to spite her.

The healer sighed and backed away.

I realized I'd carried the sword I'd picked up into the throne room with me, and I put it down before kneeling in front of him. "What happened? How'd you even get hurt? Weren't you supposed to say here? I told you to stay here. You should've been safe behind these walls, Ronan! There's an army between you and the vampires." Dammit, I should've known better than to leave his side. Of course he would do something stupid the minute I turned my back.

"I did," he protested. "At least, until we got news of the reinforcements. I was trying to go over the ramparts to get to the beacon on the western tower. I was lucky I wasn't two steps farther along the wall. A big boulder smashed into it. All I got was a stray arrow and a few bruises from the fall."

"Most of which have already been healed," Mab said. "But it could have been a lot worse. I told him not to go."

"Probably why he went," I mumbled and grabbed an alcohol wipe from the pack on the floor to dab a wound on the side of his head.

He hissed and jerked away.

"Don't be a baby," I said.

Ronan caught my arm and pushed it away. "Let the healers handle it. No offense, Callie, but you're about as gentle as a bull."

He was right, so I relinquished his care to the healer

standing patiently by and turned my attention to the two queens. "If he's not seriously hurt, why am I here?"

"We were hoping to get an update on the situation," Titania said. She folded her hands and put them in her lap as if she were sitting at a table, waiting for tea to be served.

I looked back to where Kai and William stood by the door. They had the same exhausted look in their eyes as the rest of the soldiers, and Kai's armor had new dents.

"Basically," I said, "we're fucked if we don't do something bold. They've pushed our forces back behind the walls and reinforced their lines. The only saving grace we've got right now is the palace walls. As long as they hold, we'll be fine, but we won't last through a long siege, not with those trebuchets out there."

"We could try the portal trick again," Kai suggested, moving away from the door a few steps, his hand on his sheathed sword. "They've played their ace and won't have any further reinforcements. If we come out behind them, we can push again, just as we did before, except this time, we target those trebuchets."

I shook my head. "We don't have the troops. It was a massacre out there, Kai. Judging by the numbers that made it back into the courtyard, we won't be able to do any sort of push without more boots on the ground."

Ronan cleared his throat. "That's why I was trying to get to the beacon. It's magic. If it gets lit, it sends a call for aid to every fae anywhere."

Mab frowned. "But all the fae are here."

I saw what he was getting at. "All the winter and the summer fae soldiers are here. There are still some independent fae out there who might be able to help, and we could pull some of the troops you left behind."

"Leaving the winter palace unguarded?" Mab shook her head. "No. I won't do it."

"We need every body we can get." Ronan put a hand on his mother's shoulder. "No one is asking you to leave the palace completely unguarded. If you can spare even a few fresh soldiers, it might make a difference."

Titania stood. "It's a pointless argument since the beacon is now unreachable. That whole section of the wall collapsed into rubble. The only reason the vampires aren't pouring in through the hole is that it stands on a sheer cliff. Getting to the beacon would mean walking over unstable ruins with a two-hundred-foot drop on one side and an army of vampires on the other. You'd be visible to everyone, easy pickings for anyone who wanted to take the shot, and that's to say nothing of the tower." She went to a table that had been set up in the throne room to hold the battle maps we'd been looking at earlier.

Ronan grabbed his side and stood on wobbly legs. He almost went back down, but between Mab and me, we kept him on his feet. "Thanks," he muttered and limped over to the table full of maps. "There has to be another way."

"There is," Kai said and joined us at the table.

Titania blinked. "There is? Why don't I know about it?"

Kai smiled. "Because I didn't want you to know. Do you remember the reconstruction project you put me in charge of five years ago?"

Titania looked at the ceiling, deep in thought for a moment. "The sewage project? But the sewers don't run under the west tower. That's all storage and special event space. There are no quarters in that tower, hence no sewers."

"But that doesn't mean there are no passages." Kai waved his hand and the three-dimensional map shifted, zooming in on the space between the main palace and the western tower and then dropping underground. "It's not in the official plans because it's not officially there. See, the western tower was mostly empty, and not on any direct patrol routes. You certainly never went there, so it was the perfect place for…discreet rendezvous."

I raised an eyebrow at my brother. "You're telling me you had a special tunnel built underground for your booty calls?"

Kai's grin widened as Titania's jaw dropped, apparently shocked that her son would do such a thing. It didn't surprise me one bit. He wasn't as smooth as he thought he was.

My brother laughed. "Well, when you put it that way, I guess it's easier to explain. Look, it only tacked a small number onto the project as a whole. I promise I didn't drain the treasury for it."

Titania crossed her arms. "You and I are going to have a very serious conversation after all this is over, young man!"

I put my hands on the table and leaned over the model. "Where is the entrance to the tunnel?"

"That's the only problem." Kai moved the model around again, zooming in on a set of stairs in the courtyard—the one that had been crushed by the giant boulder. "The entrance was under this set of stairs, but—"

"A boulder from one of the trebuchets smashed the staircase." I sighed and stood back up. "Great, and I bet there wasn't a secondary entrance? What about portaling in there?"

Ronan shook his head. "Won't work. The interior masonry of towers like that generally includes spells to keep portals from functioning. It's a failsafe measure to keep people from zapping themselves anywhere they want."

"What's that there?" Mab pointed to a narrow space near the tunnel Kai had shown us.

"That?" Kai zoomed the model in more. "That's a ventilation chamber. It runs parallel to the tunnel for a while, and there was an access point between the two spaces from when I did the construction, but it's long since been sealed. You could get in through the catacombs below, but I don't know how you'd get from the vent into the tunnel, and even if you did, it could have collapsed after the boulder fell."

"How is the maintenance door sealed?" I asked.

Kai shrugged. "It was encased in concrete. I suppose you could break that down, but it would take a while, and we don't know when the vampires will try to come over the walls next. I'm sure they're regrouping as we speak."

Concrete is just a mixture of cement, water, sand, and gravel, I thought. It was porous, which meant there were teeny-tiny spaces for water to get in. If I could hit it with the same magic I used to freeze vampires, I might be able to shatter it just as easily. "I can get through the door," I said, nodding with certainty. "It'll probably be loud and attract attention when I hit it with my magic, but I can do it if you get me to the catacombs."

"You'll go, then?" Titania asked with a deeper frown.

Ronan put his hand gently on my arm. "Callie, you realize this is a suicide mission, and we don't know for certain anyone will answer."

"As long as there's a chance, we have to try, don't we?"

He took his hand away and nodded, although he didn't seem happy about letting me go. What choice did we have? It was either light the beacon and hope someone out there still cared enough to come help or wait out the siege until the vampires got tired of letting us squirm and fought their way in. I'd rather do something than sit on my hands and wait for death to come for the people I'd come to care about and me. If that meant crawling through yet another sewer, so be it.

CHAPTER NINETEEN

I took stock of everything I had access to. There weren't any bullets left, and I had discarded the gun anyway. The Kevlar I'd put on had several new tears, but overall still seemed to be in good enough shape to make it. I patched it with some duct tape Kai found in a drawer. Never underestimate the power of duct tape.

For weapons, I had the sword I'd carried into the throne room. It would have to do, although I wasn't professionally trained to use it by any means. I figured as long as I remembered to stick the pointy end in the bad guy, I'd be okay so long as I didn't run into any professional duelists. I didn't have any accelerant left to light the beacon, but I did have a few matches from my trip to the vampire encampment. I tucked those into my pocket for safekeeping.

Kai left the throne room and returned with an oil lamp, some new stakes for any vampires I might run into, and a couple of knives he'd found. They were a little dull and not weighted well, but they'd work in a pinch.

"Are you sure you want to do this?" Kai asked me as I slid the knives into anywhere I could conceal them. "I mean, you might die. Doesn't that bother you?"

"I could die in my sleep, but that doesn't keep me awake at night." I slid the last knife through a belt loop and patted it. Hopefully, it'd stay in place. "Besides, even if that's a possibility, I don't plan on it being the outcome. I plan on living long enough to be a pain in everyone's ass for years to come."

Kai laughed at that and nodded. "Good attitude. I like it. Careful, though. You almost sound like me."

"Well, we *are* twins."

"Speaking of that, I figured I shouldn't let my big sister go into uncharted territory alone. I'm coming with you."

I looked up from adjusting my belt. "Kai…"

He held up a hand, halting my protests with a single gesture. "Hear me out, Callie. I'm the only one who knows those tunnels, and in the dark, it'll be easy for you to get turned around, especially in the catacombs. I know exactly where the door you're looking for is. Trust me when I say you could walk right past it and never know. Since time is of the essence, it's better that I tag along. Besides, you're not going to turn down assistance from the best swordsman in summer, are you?" He patted the sword at his side, grinning from ear to ear.

"What does our mother think about sending both of her children on this suicide mission?"

Kai winked at me. "I won't tell her if you don't." He glanced past me. "I'll meet you in the hall when you're ready."

Kai made a quick exit to avoid Ronan, who was approaching fast.

"He got out of here quick when you came over," I said and finished tightening my belt.

"I don't think he trusts me, which is just fine. I don't trust him either."

"I don't blame you. He did kidnap you." I finished getting everything in place and took a step back. "How do I look? Think this'll make it on the runway for fall fashion week?" I was a hodgepodge of duct tape, Kevlar, and pointy objects, hardly the sort of outfit anyone would take photos of.

Ronan laughed. "Well, fashion is not about functionality. I think it's perfect as long as it gets the job done and keeps you safe." He fiddled nervously with his hands. "Callie, about what I was trying to say earlier. About what I want us to be."

I braced myself for another awkward conversation, but it didn't come. Instead, Ronan stepped in close—too close. If it'd been anyone else, I might've backed away, but we were comfortable at this distance, weren't we? If that was true, why was my heart pounding out a quick-time march in my ears.

His eyes met mine, and my breath caught in my throat, trapped there. "What do *you* want?"

I don't know which one of us leaned in first. Looking back, it was impossible to tell. At the moment, it seemed like we leaned into each other, our lips meeting somewhere in the middle. It lasted only a second, barely long enough to register that it'd happened. It was over before I knew it. If not for the warm tingle on my lips after, I would have thought I'd imagined the whole thing.

He stood there for a long moment, waiting for a reaction, I think. Waiting for me to yell at him or reject him or something.

I reminded myself that I should breathe and inhaled shakily. "Don't think that means I'm going to stop nagging you about safety measures."

A smile finally sprouted on his face. "Wouldn't dream of it. Now go save the kingdom."

I took a step back, shifting my gaze from Ronan to Mab, who waited on the other side of the table. She glared at me, her lips pressed into a pale, thin line and her arms crossed. Her eye twitched. The winter queen obviously didn't approve of her son getting involved with me, but what could she do about it? I could almost see the wheels turning in her head and the smoke coming out of her ears as she started making plans to cause trouble between us.

But not now. Now, she stepped out of my way and let me pass, even though I could feel her angry eyes boring into the back of my head as I made my way to the door.

I met Kai in the hallway. He wore a smug grin. "Ready to go?"

"You can wipe that grin off your face," I snapped. "I don't want to hear anything about what just happened."

"I didn't say anything."

"Not a word, Kai."

He mimicked zipping his lips and throwing the key over his shoulder before shoving his hands into his pockets. I was glad about the silence as we made our way through the palace. Outside, the sounds of people hammering things and moving equipment around echoed through the courtyard, along with voices shouting orders. The taunting cries of vampires rallying in the small clearing between the palace and the forest was a steady accompaniment in the background.

"How long do you think we have before they come over the walls?" I asked Kai.

He shrugged. "They'll probably get the trebuchets up and running again shortly and keep firing them through the day. If they plan to come forward with terms of surrender, I expect it'll be either tonight or tomorrow morning. They'll want to batter us into submission first."

I snorted and shook my head. "Terms of surrender, my ass. It won't matter if the fae agree to their terms or not. They're going to kill everyone. Vaughn isn't the sort to leave survivors behind."

"We'd better hope this beacon trick of yours works, then." Kai gestured to a door.

I opened it. A set of stairs spiraled down into darkness on the other side.

He held out the lantern, which illuminated one, maybe two steps. "The royal catacombs."

I took the lantern from him and started down the stairs at a quick but steady pace. "And here I thought fae were functionally immortal."

"'Immortal' doesn't mean impervious to poison, sharp objects, or iron." He counted on his fingers as we descended. "Fae can die, just not of old age. Considering the inner workings of the courts, plenty of us have been assassinated over the years."

"You say 'us' as if you're one of them." I raised the

lantern higher, but it didn't do much good. The stairs seemed to go down forever.

"Granted, we are half-fae, but no one here looks down on me for that. Fae tend to be much more accepting than humans, who can't seem to work out they're all just one big mess, no matter what walk of life they're in."

I suppressed a chuckle. "Isn't that the truth?"

The stairs finally ended, spilling into a large, curved stone room. Though it had been sweltering-hot above, even with magic pumping cool air through the palace, it was cold in the catacombs. If I hadn't been wrapped tight in Kevlar and layers of duct tape, I would have been shivering.

At first glance, there wasn't much to look at. It just seemed like a round chamber. Sealed shelves bore the names of the dead, no one I recognized. The smaller room led us into a larger chamber with sealed shelves four or five high and ten deep. More tunnels opened in all four directions, curving deeper into the catacombs. I imagined that there were more rooms like that one farther in, each as full.

I whistled and the sound carried through the room, bouncing off the curved walls and shooting back at me to make it sound as if five people whistled, not one. "How many bodies are down here?"

"Every fae in the summer court who's ever died rests here," Kai whispered. "They say that one day all the dead will rise again, but I think that's just superstition. Every culture has some sort of afterlife myth. This is theirs. The fae never say their loved ones have died. They're only resting."

I shivered. Over the years, I'd been in hundreds of graveyards and a few morgues, but never beneath the earth where the dead were supposed to be. It felt wrong, being in here with them—as if we were intruding on their space. I wanted to get out of there as fast as possible. "Which way?"

Kai pointed to the corridor on the right.

I went to it and stepped into yet another low tunnel with a rounded ceiling. There were more shelves on either side, but I didn't stop to look at them. I had been right about there being more big rooms like the first. The tunnel led into an identical room that was only slightly less full. Kai took me to the tunnel on the opposite side of the room this time and into yet another big room. We passed through six of them before we were through the catacombs, and I'd only seen a small portion of them. I was glad I'd brought him down there with me. Without a guide, I would've wandered in circles for hours without ever finding my way.

At the end of the longest corridor, I saw a light. It was dim and pale blue, like moonlight. I passed Kai as I went toward it, and he grabbed me by the collar, halting me.

I turned around and took a swing at him, which he ducked. "What the hell? Don't scare me like that. I thought you were a vampire!"

"Liar." He stuck his tongue out at me. "If you thought I was a vampire, I'd be dead or close to it. You don't go easy on your enemies." Kai gestured to a white circle on the wall. "Here's your door."

I held the lantern up to it and frowned. "Doesn't look very big. It'll be a tight fit."

"I warned you about that, but I think we can make it one at a time."

"Stand back." I waited for him to take a couple of steps back before I placed my palm flat on the concrete. At first, nothing happened when I called my magic, I couldn't wrangle it into submission and make it do what I wanted.

Come on. Please work! I closed my eyes and focused everything I had on the wall ahead of me, imagining it under a microscope with its porous openings and the little mismatched rocks. Then I felt the chill of ice on my fingertips, but the power refused to jump into the wall.

"Dammit!" I shouted and drew my fist back, slamming it as hard as I could into the wall.

In retrospect, that was a stupid move. If I'd been a normal person, or even if my magic hadn't come out when it did, I would have broken my hand. Luckily, my power surged to the surface with the punch and the whole wall iced over. When my knuckles hit it, it shattered into big chunks of cement and brick and fell with puffs of dust and noise.

For a minute, the narrow hall was too clogged with debris, ice, and dust to see. I heard Kai coughing a short distance away, but it seemed like the wrong direction. After a few seconds, I realized that was because the impact had knocked me on my ass and I was staring at the ceiling, completely disoriented.

Kai appeared in my field of vision, waving dust away from his face. "Quite a performance," he remarked, holding out a hand.

"Thanks." I took his offered hand and pulled myself to my feet. One of the biggest chunks had landed on the ground only inches to the right of my head. If I'd fallen just a bit to the right, it would have crushed my skull, and this would all be over. I stared at the hunk of frozen concrete. "Do you think they heard that?"

As if in answer, a chorus of voices echoed from whatever was on the other side of the sealed doorway.

Kai and I exchanged glances, and he drew his sword. "You ready?"

"Are you kidding? I was born ready." I took out two of the stakes I had. "Last one to the fight's a rotten egg," I shouted and rushed into the narrow opening I'd just created.

CHAPTER TWENTY

The air on the other side was much less musty, and the walls had been constructed of something other than old brick. I couldn't tell what it was, but the hallway I'd blasted into was only slightly less nice than the rest of the palace. There weren't any decorations on the walls, but there had been little oil lamps, which I had shattered with my blast of ice. The carpet was ruined. Water trickled down the hall from all the melting ice.

We crept down the hall with our weapons at the ready, listening to the vampires scurrying around in the dark ahead. Every sound seemed louder, from my breathing to my heartbeat pounding in my ears. My palms were damp. Every footfall echoed through the hall.

I didn't spot the first one for quite a while. He was crawling along the ceiling, clinging to it by his claws. His eyes finally gave him away. They caught the light reflecting off our lanterns and cast them back like cat eyes. A bright green sheen passed over them, making it seem as if they were glowing.

Slowly, I set the lantern down, waiting for him to come close enough to attack. Two more suddenly barreled down the narrow hall, armed with swords. I let Kai step ahead of me to take care of them, and he batted one aside. The creature hit the wall and bounced off right onto my wooden stake. The other got a chest full of Kai's sword, and vampire ash rained down like confetti. The one that had been crawling along the ceiling dropped a few feet ahead with a hiss and a splash. Kai ran up before the vampire could rise and kicked him in the chin. He went up like a cartoon, splashing down into the running water to land on his back. Kai drove the sword into the vampire's chest, and that was the last of him.

Without another word, we raced down the narrow corridor to the second group of vampires, maybe twenty more yards in. Kai swung his sword and took the arm off one, missing his swing at the head. It was a dangerous mistake. The vampire launched off the ground, bounced off the low ceiling, and landed between us. I lifted my stake to drive it into him, but he swiped at me with his claws. Three burning lines tore across the inside of my right arm and scraped over my chest armor, missing my face by mere inches. I kicked him back and stabbed him with the wooden stake.

I spun and found myself fending off blows from yet another vampire. He clawed at me, forcing me back down the hall. I ducked, barely avoiding being scratched. After a few swings, he launched himself at me. I ducked and let him jump over me. He landed, confused, with his back to me. Before he could turn around, I gave him a push, sending him off balance. He fell, and I staked him while he was down.

Two more sprang onto the walls, moving around Kai. He tried to turn to engage them, but another set came down the hall, charging on all fours. While he dealt with them, I finally resorted to drawing the sword. I wasn't trained to use it like Kai, but some part of me seemed to know what I was doing. I swung it left and right, missing both swings but managing to fend off the vampires. One darted in close enough that I could grab his outstretched arm, and I sent a pulse of magic into him, freezing him solid. With one push, I knocked him over, and he shattered on the floor.

"See, why can't it work like that every time?" I complained as I took a step back. Somehow, more vampires had gotten behind me. I could see their eyes shining in the darkness. My back bumped against Kai's. "How're you doing, brother?"

"Bit of a workout, but I was due for one. You?"

"I really hate bloodsuckers."

Kai laughed. "That makes two of us."

We pushed off each other and rushed toward our opponents. There were three vampires on my side, and he had four to deal with. One of mine had a big shield, and he ran with it out in front of him. There was no room in the narrow space to maneuver around the shield, so I put my hand out and snagged it when he came close. He tried to bite my other arm, but he couldn't twist far enough to get a good chomp. I touched the shield and called my magic one more time. The wood swelled up like a balloon before shattering into splinters, leaving him and his fellow vampires exposed.

I dropped the sword, and with a shout, grabbed their heads and slammed them together. They staggered apart, dazed. I drew two knives and plunged one into each vampire's chest. They didn't go in very far at first, so I shifted my weight and forced them in. The vamps hissed and struggled the whole time, but couldn't move well enough to get to me.

They exploded into ash clouds, and my knives clattered to the ground. I bent over to pick them up before turning around to see how Kai was doing.

There was one vampire left, which had him pinned to the wall. He was holding the thing off him by grasping his forehead and jaw, but my brother was losing ground. The vampire wasn't paying any attention to me, however, so I had plenty of time to put my knives away and pick up the sword.

"A little help here?" Kai ground out.

"I'm coming." I thrust the sword into the vampire's chest from the side. He went down like all the others.

Kai let out a heavy sigh of relief and gripped his chest. "Cutting it a little close there, Callie."

I held out my hand and pulled him away from the wall. "Ready to go light this fire?"

He nodded. "Exit's just ahead."

We ran forward, keeping our weapons handy in case we ran into more vampires. Luckily we didn't, which was a good thing considering I was very tired. If I had to fight any more vampires, I might fall over from exhaustion.

Stairs appeared in the dim light ahead, and I let out a

relieved breath. I'd never been so happy to see stairs in my life. We climbed them in a crouch, carefully inching around every curve in case there were more vampires. We must've taken care of all the vamps Vaughn had stationed in that tower, though, because not a single one appeared between us and the top of the tower.

Off the final landing was a large round room with what looked like a bird's nest in the center. We stayed low as we approached since we were open to the elements up there, and one wrong move would alert the vampire army to our presence. All we had to do was light the fire and get back out before the place was swarmed with vampires.

I touched the wood and cursed.

"What?" asked Kai, creeping closer.

"It's wet. Matches will never get this thing lit."

He smirked and pushed up his sleeves. "Leave this to me." Kai extended both hands toward the wet wood and formed a glowing ball of orange fire in his palms. In a flash of bright light and heat, the fire coalesced into a short, intense beam that struck the wood and set it ablaze despite it being wet.

The fire soared high, casting bright light over the entire area and out into the night. Every vampire within five miles probably saw the fire spring up, and all of them now knew where we were.

"Come on," I shouted and ran for the stairs. "We need to get out of here before they block our exit."

Our footsteps echoed through the stone stairwell as we rushed toward the hall where we'd find our exit waiting. Something scurried along the exterior of the tower, claws scraping loudly over solid stone and concrete. As I rushed past one of the slit windows, a hand reached through it. Glowing vampire eyes appeared in the slit and hissed loudly.

Kai cut off the vampire's arm. "Run!"

I was already running at full speed, but it wasn't enough to head off the vampires. They crashed through the ground floor entrance to the tower, pouring in like water. I backed up, but there was nowhere to go in that direction either. They'd climbed the tower and started down the stairs toward us.

Once again, Kai and I were back to back, fighting off vampires, only this time we were exhausted and sore. I only had a few stakes left, not nearly enough to win this fight. Even with the knives, I didn't think we stood a chance. There were too many vampires, and they were coming at us from all directions. Still, if I was going to die, I wanted to go down fighting.

I drew a knife and slashed at the first vamp stupid enough to come close, pushing him back. The next one got a blast of ice to the face, then I kicked him into his fellow vamps. They buckled under the weight of catching him, then let him go. He tumbled down the stairs before striking the rear wall and shattering.

Kai had much better luck with his sword, fighting two or three of them at once. The only failing was the narrow, curved stairway we were on. He couldn't advance since they kept coming, and the more he cut down, the more ash he had to navigate through. It quickly got deep enough to make him wary of his footing.

The ice I was throwing around didn't help the situation. I turned a few times and blasted vampires on his side that were getting too close. After the magic sat for a moment, all that ice began to melt, and it had nowhere to go but down, creating a slick river. The ash turned into sludgy mud, sticking to everything. I tried not to think about what was caking my shoes and my arm, but it was impossible not to. The thought that I was wearing something that had been alive a short while ago made my stomach turn.

Two vampires jumped at me. One grabbed my arm and wrenched it behind me, twisting my wrist, and I had no choice but to drop the knife I was wielding. I kicked at him, but the other grabbed me. Kai spun with his sword. I thought for sure he would accidentally take my head off, but he only got the vampire I'd just kicked. I elbowed the one holding me, or tried to, but couldn't get enough momentum to land a decent blow. I grabbed his arm and tried to call my magic, but it didn't respond; all I got was a trickle of power. I'd reached my limit and would need some time to recharge before I could use another spell.

The vampires crowded in, impatient to get a bite of my brother and me.

We were doomed. I squeezed my eyes shut and tried to shut out the sound of them scratching and salivating all around me. If you'd asked me how I thought I'd die six months ago, trapped in a tower in a magical realm and killed by vampires wouldn't have been at the top of the list. Yet there I was, facing my demise. I wondered if they'd find enough of me to bury. How would Sam react when they told them? If anyone got out of Faerie to let them know. How long would it be before anyone realized I wasn't coming back?

And what the hell was that sound?

It started low and steady, like distant waves crashing on a sandy beach. The longer it went on, however, the louder it became. After a few moments, my eyes snapped open. Voices. What I was hearing was the rallying cry of the reinforcements we'd called for.

The vampires paused, turning their heads as their trumpets sounded. They were being called back to battle, and Vaughn would need every one of them if he wanted to have a chance of repelling our fresh forces. I didn't think he stood a chance. Independent fae didn't get to be independent just by asking. They had to be powerful, strong enough that Mab and Titania didn't mess with them. One good independent fae was probably worth ten of Titania's soldiers, and they wouldn't be tired.

The vampire holding me relaxed his grip. I seized the opportunity and reared my head back. On instinct, he let me go, staggering back to grip his broken nose. Before he could react further, Kai shouted and drove his sword through the vampire's chest. I staked him with the knife for good measure, and we kicked him against the others, who were already retreating.

Kai and I stood on the stairway, watching them run back to battle.

"Am I crazy?" Kai asked, "or did that just work?"

I patted his arm. "I think it worked. Come on. It's not over yet. We still have to win this. Let's go kick the vampires off your land."

CHAPTER TWENTY-ONE

Pockets of fighting continued throughout the area around and in front of the palace for another twenty minutes or so. Some vampires had gotten caught before they could retreat, and the fae were making short work of them. We passed several fights as we made our way back, all of them two fae on one vampire, usually working out in favor of the fae.

It was all over by the time Kai and I made it out of the tower, though. We walked through the empty spaces full of ash and tired faces. You'd think I'd be used to seeing fighting and death considering I'd been in the military, but this was different somehow. More personal. I knew the enemy, or at least who was commanding them. I'd met him in person.

Vaughn had escaped, though, which meant the war wasn't over. He'd spend some time licking his wounds and rebuilding his numbers to come back again and again until one side wore out the other and they finally settled on peace. Or until one side wiped out the other. Either way, this wasn't over.

Knowing that didn't make me feel hopeful. I was numb and tired from being awake for so long. My limbs ached from fighting. My stomach growled and twisted itself into knots, reminding me it'd been a while since I'd eaten. I didn't know which I wanted to do first: eat, sleep, or take the world's longest bath.

Before I could do any of those things, however, I needed to get back to the throne room to check on Ronan and the two queens. Leaving them alone together for any length of time seemed like it might lead to more fighting breaking out, and I didn't want the fragile truce to fall apart so soon.

Mab and Titania were in the hall outside the throne room when I arrived. Ronan limped along behind them, leaning heavily on the wall. The healers might've tended to his wounds, but that didn't mean he wouldn't be sore for a while. Fighting exacted a toll, both mentally and physically; we'd all need a few days to recover after this.

After making sure everyone was okay, it was time to set up the throne room for whatever ceremony Mab and Titania wanted to hold. It seemed there was no rest for the wicked. I started moving chairs alongside the palace servants, only to be stopped by William with a hand on my shoulder.

"You should rest while you can. Let them do this," he said.

I shifted my grip on the stack of three wooden chairs and glanced around. The fresh-faced servants scurried around with more energy than I had on a good day. They hadn't seen battle, but rather had holed up somewhere deep in the palace to wait out all the fighting. They moved with nervous energy and a little excitement, happy to be free from where they'd been trapped.

I put the chairs down. "Yeah. I think you're right."

There weren't any proper bedrooms available for a nap. That floor had been damaged when one of the trebuchets flung a big rock at it. Instead, William brought me to the barracks in the rear of the palace. It was a large, rectangular building, connected to the palace by an underground walkway. It boasted several rooms on the second floor for sleeping, but all of them were empty when I arrived. William also told me there were showers and a kitchen if I was hungry. The bunks there were stacked three high and four deep, offering plenty of space for me to catch a little nap. Even as tired as I was, I wanted to clean up first, so I went to the nearest shower.

Stripping off the Kevlar and various bits of armor revealed more bruises than I thought I'd gotten in the fight. My skin was a rainbow of purple, gray, and yellow marks, but nothing was broken. Part of me knew I should've reported to a healer to make sure, but I reasoned that nothing felt painful enough to be a broken bone, and I was honestly too tired to care. The longest shower in the world was going to have to wait until I was awake enough to stand for more than three minutes.

I turned on the water and stood under it, leaning against the wall. If not for the steaming-hot water burning my back, I would have fallen asleep right there. There wasn't any soap or shampoo, so it wasn't much of a shower, just a chance to rinse off the blood, mud, and ash from the fight. Still, I'd take what I could get.

Cleaner, I dragged myself back to the nearest bunk and crawled into it. Normally, I'd complain about the hard mattress, the itchy blanket, or the tight quarters, but I was too tired to care. The tiny bunk with its wool blanket felt like heaven. I curled into a tight ball and fell asleep in less than a minute.

I don't know how long I slept, but I remember dreaming I was back at the Kloud9 factory, doing rounds. I wandered around in the dark with a flickering flashlight, moving the unreliable beam over mannequins that were in different positions each time I looked at them. I never saw them move, but I had the uneasy feeling they were just waiting to step out of the darkness and grab me.

Someone shook me awake a short while later, and I had to stop myself from swinging at them. Ronan put his hands up defensively. "Do you always take a swing at people who wake you up?"

I grunted and sat up, rubbing sleep from my eyes. "No. Normally, it's my alarm clock, and I pick it up and smash it against the wall. You should see my bedroom with its pile of broken alarm clocks in one corner. I keep them there as a warning to the others."

Ronan tilted his head to the side with a frown.

I sighed. "It's a joke. How long have I been asleep?"

"Maybe an hour?" He eased onto the cot across from me. "Mab and Titania want to do a joint ceremony to thank all the independent fae. They are going to recognize you specifically, but I wanted to make sure you were feeling up to that. Are you?"

"Yeah, I guess." I swung my legs over the side of the cot and stretched, cracking my back in four places. "As long as nobody is expecting me to dress up." The fae didn't have much in the way of regular clothes lying around the palace, but one of the servants had been nice enough to grab me a t-shirt and a pair of black sweats that fit well enough if I pulled the drawstring tight.

Ronan laughed. "You're the hero of the hour. I think you can wear what you want to your own ceremony. Come on." He extended his hand.

I took it and slid out of the bunk. The floor was cold, and I remembered I'd taken off my socks and shoes. Grumbling, I grabbed both and put them back on before walking with Ronan out of the barracks.

The hallway leading from the barracks to the throne room section of the palace was buzzing with activity. Servants rushed past with cleaning supplies and random people seemed to be standing around, picking things up or carrying them from one place to another. It should've felt chaotic, but it didn't. The fae seemed to know what to do after a big battle. Each had their tasks and went about completing them as quickly and quietly as possible. I remembered having that sort of certainty back in my military days. It was all but gone now. There was no playbook for being an independent fae, the bodyguard for the winter prince and the daughter of the summer queen all at once. I didn't feel like any of those things. I was just me—Callie Hart. That hadn't changed just because I'd found out who my parents were, and that I was half-fae.

We stopped outside the throne room, which had its giant doors propped open. Soldiers stood on either side.

William and Kai were on the dais with Titania and Mab, who somehow both had thrones, although Titania's was a little bigger and nicer than Mab's. They must've kept a spare throne around for visiting monarchs. I wondered when Mab had last been to the summer court. Given their fighting, it must've been a while.

"We'll wait here," Ronan said.

I looked around. "Wait for what?"

"For them to introduce us and summon you to the front. I'll escort you." He flashed a big smile. "Fae are big on formalities, you know. Don't forget to bow when you approach the throne. First to Titania, since this is technically her court and Mab is visiting, and then to Mab. If you forget, people will whisper about it for ages, and you'll never shrug it off. We fae like to gossip almost as much as we like formalities."

I frowned. "Now I see why you don't want to spend much time at court."

He nodded.

In the throne room, Titania stood and began a speech, thanking everyone for coming and for their bravery and so on. It sounded like every other speech by a medal-awarding politician I'd ever heard, so I tuned it out. I was more interested in scanning the faces in the crowd, trying to learn what I could about the people gathered there. Some of them I recognized from the last few times I'd been to the winter court or summer court, but others were strangers. When they were all crowded into the throne room like sardines in a tin can, it was impossible to tell who was a member of the summer court, who was with winter, and who was an independent. Everyone looked like they belonged there. Everyone, of course, except for me. I hadn't taken the time to put on nice clothes or do my hair. Instead, I'd come to court wearing sweatpants, with my hair a mess from sleeping on it wet. Suddenly self-conscious, I ran my hands through my hair to get it to lay flat.

"Callie Hart, please come forward." I almost fell over when William's voice boomed.

Ronan's arm tightened around mine. "Start on the left foot."

Somehow, I forgot my right from my left at that moment and went on the right, which made for awkward walking until I figured out how to match his pace.

Walking up the aisle in silence with hundreds of strangers staring at me made my skin crawl and my throat constrict. I imagined myself missing a step or catching the carpet and falling flat on my face and everyone bursting out into laughter. That didn't happen, though, and I somehow made it to the thrones in what felt like a single step. I stood there for a moment before I remembered what Ronan had told me to do, then bent in half awkwardly twice. I could practically hear the indignation in Mab's sigh.

Titania smiled. "Approach and kneel."

I did as she instructed, climbing to the top stair of the platform and slowly going to my knees. The stone made my kneecaps ache.

"Callie Hart," said Titania. "Where do I begin? Before you came into our lives, we thought we were content, separated as we were. You, however, have shown us that true strength lies in working together. Together, we repelled an army of vampires, a feat which would not have been possible without your aid, and the aid of all independent fae. Today we thank you for your bravery in the face of danger and your fast thinking. Your ability to unite two monarchs who had become strangers has saved us."

I lifted my head slightly. "If I may speak freely?"

"Of course, my dear."

"Nobody's been saved." I waited for surprised gasps or for someone to protest, but all I got in return was Mab's deep frown intensifying, so I continued. "We won the battle, but it's too early to say we've won the war. Vaughn is still out there. He's going to rally and strike harder, again and again like a hammer until either he wins or we do. This was one battle. More are coming until he's been dealt with."

Titania nodded solemnly. "Our forces will hunt him to the ends of the Earth and beyond if need be. We too will rally our forces and strike proactively. There is nowhere he can go where we will not sniff him out. Rest assured, the vampire threat will be dealt with swiftly and decisively, once this day of celebration is done. For now, we must acknowledge that summer, and by extension, all of Faerie, has been saved. The independent fae came when called, and for that, they have our endless gratitude. However, you, Callie, were instrumental in the success of this battle, and we must recognize your efforts."

I shook my head. "It wasn't just me. Kai should be recognized too. He fought alongside me. Without his help, I would not have made it to the tower."

Mab pushed up from her throne. "Winter recognizes the assistance of the summer knight in this matter. As such, the gratitude of the winter court and Queen Mab extends to Sir Kai of the summer court."

Kai nodded from his place by the throne. "Just doing my job."

Titania turned back to me with an even bigger smile, folding her hands. "We thank you, Callie, and offer you the only gift we have to give: a boon from each court. Ask whatever you will, and if it is within our power to grant it, you shall have it."

I swallowed. Anything I wanted? Mab and Titania were powerful queens, and they had each written me a blank check. Maybe it was best I put those away for a rainy day. Who knew what the future held? I'd need their help sometime for sure, and I couldn't think of anything I wanted at the moment. At least, nothing besides another shower and a longer nap.

"May I request the boons be granted at a later time?" I asked.

Mab sighed. "Of course, child. No one expects you to use up your favors in one day."

"Good," I said, relieved. "Because honestly, the only thing I want right now more than a nap is a hot meal."

Titania laughed. "And you shall have it. Stay, and I will have a banquet prepared in your honor."

As hungry as I was, I wasn't up to a banquet. That would mean schmoozing with more royals and dealing with crowds. I would have been fine with a pizza and a spot on the floor in Ronan's guest room. I looked at Ronan, hoping my expression communicated that I wanted him to bail me out.

He cleared his throat and stepped forward like the

angel he was. "I'm afraid a banquet will have to wait. Callie and I are needed elsewhere. We must see to my estate on Earth."

Titania nodded. "Another time, then. Will you at least accept a proper send-off as you return home?"

"Absolutely," I said.

"Then rise." She reached for my hands, helping me to my feet. I thought she'd let me go after that, but she pulled me into a hug. "I'm sorry about before," she whispered. "I'll make it up to you."

Before I could answer, she spun me around. The crowd cheered, and Ronan took my arm to march me down. Our departure was a blur, but I was even more exhausted than before.

CHAPTER TWENTY-TWO

Ronan made a portal in the courtyard while a dozen fae watched, clapping and cheering. Everyone I met along the way stopped me to thank me. I felt like I was suddenly a celebrity, although I was sure half the people who shook my hand didn't know who I was beyond my name and what Titania had said in the throne room. They were just happy to have won, and since they'd all been told they had me to thank for it, they extended that happiness to me. I tried to accept their thanks and congratulations with grace, but I was not used to having that much praise heaped on me at once. All I wanted was to go back to the mansion and hide for a bit.

Stepping through the portal to Ohio was a relief. It was a quiet afternoon on the other side. Birds sang in the trees and cars rushed by on the roads beyond the trees. The quiet murmur of the city filled the air, making it feel like home.

But the ground seemed to move when I put my feet on it, and I lost my balance.

"Careful!" Ronan said and caught me before I could fall.

"Thanks. I must be more tired than I thought."

"Makes sense. That would be hard on anybody, what you just went through. I was only in a very small skirmish, and I'm worn out. I don't know how you did all that and stayed on your feet as long as you did."

I waited for him to let me go, but he didn't. He caught my eyes and started to lean in more for another kiss. I turned my head and wriggled out of his grasp with a frustrated sigh.

"What?" he asked. "What's wrong? Did I overstep?"

"No, it's not that." I crossed my arms and paced for a moment, trying to find the right words. "I just don't know if it'd work, you and me. I'm your employee. Wouldn't that be weird? I don't want to pursue something that's going to turn out to be nothing because it's my job to be here. I don't know if that makes sense to you."

"It does." Ronan shrugged. "And I'm more than happy to fire you if you want."

I stopped pacing and stared at him. "What?"

"I said if the job is getting in the way, let's get rid of the job. I can promote someone else to head of security." He shrugged again.

I rolled my eyes. "Ha-ha. Very funny."

"I'm serious. You cost me a fortune." He put his hands in his pockets and strolled lazily toward the house on the other side of the tree line. "With what I would save by not paying your salary, I could afford to make it on my own without relying on my mother to make up the difference. You're the one who's been telling me all this time I should be more independent of her. I'm sure I could promote Mark and pay him half as much."

I frowned, imagining Mark as his head of security. It'd be a disaster, and they'd both be dead within the first week. Maybe not from an assassin, but because Mark wasn't pushy enough to get Ronan to listen to him. Ronan needed someone who would argue with him when it was called for and push back against all the crazy ideas he had. "If you fired me, who would save your ass from vampires every other week?"

He grinned wide. "You would. I just wouldn't have to pay you for it."

"That's not how this works, Ronan."

He turned his smile into an exaggerated frown. "Are you saying you only save me because I pay you? Do I mean nothing to you, Callie Hart, beyond the paycheck?"

I sighed, exasperated. "You know that's not what I meant! Stop twisting everything I say. It's annoying."

"Think about it." He drew his hand through the air in front of him as if illustrating a landscape. "You and I could live like royalty here. I can be the musically inclined, head in the clouds, broody artistic millionaire model. You can be my fierce warrior queen. Together, we tame the jungle that is Columbus with its steel and glass skyscrapers and plethora of college campuses!"

I couldn't help but laugh at that. "If I was going to have a kingdom, I'm not sure I'd want it to be Columbus, Ohio."

"And why not? Columbus is a fine city."

I glanced around. It was nice enough, I supposed, but it didn't fit the definition of a kingdom. "Okay, you're telling me this is where you'd center your kingdom if you were a king? Suburbia, Ohio? We're not even in Columbus proper here. You know what Ohio is famous for? Astronauts, Ronan. This state has the most people who've gone to space. You know why that is? Ohio is so damn boring, they have to go to space to escape their boredom."

He chuckled. "Well, at least we're not Michigan."

I snorted. "Spoken like a true Ohioan." We walked a short distance before I asked, "Why did you choose to live in Ohio anyway?"

Ronan slowed his pace, shrugging yet again. "Cheap real estate and boredom, I guess. Nothing happens in Ohio, as you were kind enough to point out. I suppose I was looking for somewhere to rest, a quiet place away from my mother and the politics of the court. I'm not sure I succeeded, though. Honestly, I can't complain. There's a good airport here, the people have largely left me alone, and no one bothers me. Those were my requirements when I was looking for a place and why I bought this house, so I got what I paid for, I suppose. Plus, there's all that extra room."

I stopped walking and turned to face Ronan. "You really would fire me?"

He smiled, shook his head, and rolled his eyes to the sky. "Oh, Callie. You're thinking of it the wrong way. I'm not going to fire you. You should know me better than that. But, if you chose to leave the job, or maybe take a step back, or even just a few months off to see if we can work this out and make a go of this, I wouldn't complain."

"And if I take all that time off and it doesn't work out? What then?" I leaned against a tree, arms crossed. "I come back to work for you, and we can be all awkward with each other?"

"Again, you're thinking about it the wrong way." He put a hand on the tree trunk next to me and leaned in. "You're so focused on what to do if it doesn't work out, you haven't considered the alternative. What if it does, Callie? We just saw…" His voice trailed off and he stared into the distance for a long moment. "I don't know. After what we've just been through, it seems silly to let something so small get in the way, doesn't it?"

"Life is short, right? Except it isn't for you." I slid away from the tree, pacing a few more feet into the forest. "You could live forever, and I probably won't."

He wrapped a warm arm around my shoulders and squeezed. "Then let's not think about forever, okay? This isn't a problem we have to solve right now or even this week. We'll work it out if you want, and if you don't…well, you do, don't you?"

I uncrossed my arms and turned around to find him frowning, eyes big. "Of course I do. I'd have punched you in the nose for kissing me otherwise."

That broke him. He doubled over laughing, bracing himself with one arm against the tree to keep from falling over.

I frowned. "What'd I say that was so funny?"

"Nothing," he said, standing to try to collect himself. He rubbed his eyes. "Just something only you would say. Only you would say you wanted to date me and punch me in the same breath." He winked at me.

I finally got it and smiled. He was right, and laughing provided a good release for all the tension that had built up. I went back to where he stood and put my hand in his. "Let's go back to the house and relieve Sam of duty before they start to worry."

"If they aren't already."

We walked arm in arm the rest of the way in companionable silence, listening to the birds, the city, and each other's footsteps through the grass and old leaves covering the forest floor. Ronan was right; the simplicity of something boring like a walk through the woods was nice. I'd been so busy working, I'd almost forgotten what it was like to be normal and do everyday things.

Since Ronan had come into my life, things had gone from hectic to crazy. If I wrote down everything that happened to me and put it in a book, no one would believe me. Sure, there was the occasional down day where nothing happened, but life with Ronan was one episode of insanity after another. If vampires weren't trying to kill him, there was his crazy mother to contend with. When she was absent, there was his schedule, jet-setting from one part of the globe to another for photoshoot after photoshoot. It was hard to imagine him ever settling down and having time for a real relationship, but if he was willing to take the time, why not try it? The worst that could happen was things would end badly and I'd have to find another job to escape the awkwardness. As far as poor outcomes went, that didn't seem like such a big deal. We had, after all, just survived a full-scale battle against vampires. It felt like nothing could stop us now.

We made it to the back of the house but decided to go around to the front so we didn't cause a panic when we stepped in. The front door flew open as soon as we stepped onto the porch and Sam rushed out to throw their arms around me, squeezing all the air out. My lungs burned to draw a breath but in a good way.

"You have no idea how great it is to see you!" Sam ground out through clenched teeth. "It feels like it's been forever."

"It's only been a day or so," Ronan said. He went in for a hug and instantly regretted it. When Sam squeezed him, his eyes practically bulged out of his head. He stepped back and coughed. "I trust nothing too terrible happened to the place in my absence?"

"No." Sam shook their head. "It's just that it is creepy as hell at night. I haven't slept a wink. Of course, the scary movies I watched probably didn't help. Did you know there were like twelve movies in the *Friday the Thirteenth* franchise? Of course, only three of them are any good, and only one was scary. But when you binge-watch them by yourself in a strange house…" Sam sighed. "I'm beat."

"Well," I said, rubbing a sore bruise on my ribs, "we're beat as well. I think we can all agree that the next few days are going to be as low-key as possible. I, for one, can't wait to fall into the world's hottest bath and then take the longest nap of my life."

"You haven't even told me how the battle went!" Sam swept in front of me, standing between us and the door again. "Did we win?"

"Yes, Sam," Ronan said dryly. "Sort of."

"Vaughn's still out there, but we kicked his butt," I added.

"Hell, yeah." Sam put their hand up for a high five. I

wasn't about to leave them hanging. You didn't do that to your bestie, no matter how tired you were.

A sudden huge crash made me spin around. Smoke filled the air near the front gate and a dozen black cars raced through it, speeding toward the front of the house. In the lead car, I thought I spotted a bald head and a familiar smug grin. Vaughn was making his next move.

CHAPTER TWENTY-THREE

I herded Ronan and Sam into the house and told them to go upstairs to the security room. Once they were on their way, I locked the door behind me and rushed through the house, checking windows, doors, and every possible entrance. The guards on duty would see me, and it made more sense to do it myself than call them down here. We'd sent everyone else home before we went to winter, but there were still five of us to worry about.

As many people as Vaughn had brought with him, they would have no trouble breaking through the door or windows to get in, but I wanted to make it as difficult as possible. Every minute I bought us was one more chance that Vaughn and his people wouldn't win.

If we weren't jammed and without a landline again, hopefully the guards had already called. Worst case, when they busted down the door, the security system should alert the police—if they hadn't somehow spoofed it again. The police and fire response time for this area was pretty good, but it was measured in minutes and not seconds. I had seen firsthand how fast vampires could move through a place this size. Considering how many of them there were, they would make short work of us. The only thing that would be left by the time the cops got there would be bodies and a little blood. I needed to make sure that didn't happen. Anything I could do to slow them down, I did as I ran through the house. I tossed chairs down, blocking the path to the stairs, and wedged them under doorknobs where I could.

It felt like it took forever. In the time it took me to do all that, they could have come into the house. I wondered why they hadn't, but tried not to let the thought slow me down. I'd take all the time I could get.

When I reached the stairs, Vaughn's voice came through a megaphone outside. I paused halfway up to listen. Once we went into the panic room, sound would be muffled, thanks to the insulated walls. I should've kept going, but part of me was curious about what sort of offer he planned to make.

"I know you're all in there," Vaughn said. "And you know there's no escape. My people have the house surrounded. Barred doors and locked windows will only slow us down a little, delaying the inevitable. I'm sure you think you'll be protected in your safe room with your guns and your thick walls, but I assure you that's not the case. My people will tear the house apart to get to you if need be. However, I don't think any of us wants that. All that trouble can be avoided if you just give up Callie Hart right now."

My hand slid off the railing. Me? Why would he want me? Unless this wasn't about the war at all. This was vengeance, revenge for costing him the battle and being a thorn in his side since day one. Vaughn was ready to be rid of me. I would have laughed if it wasn't so frightening.

I turned away from the front door and took the stairs two at a time. Sam and Ronan were in the security room with the guards on duty, hovering over the front door camera and watching Vaughn direct his people.

"You have three minutes to decide," Vaughn said. "If Callie Hart is not outside after that, we will come in and get her, and we will take all of you into custody. Be smart. Give us the girl, and we'll leave the rest of you alone. No one else has to die for this."

I burst into the room and stopped when eight eyes focused on me. I could feel them considering Vaughn's offer. Would they give me up to save themselves? I couldn't blame them if they did. It was my job to protect Ronan, and Sam had only gotten involved because of me. This was all my fault. If sacrificing myself would save everyone, I'd happily do it in a heartbeat. Still, if anyone decided to do it, that would hurt.

David and Ryan confirmed they didn't have signal or internet up here, so they had been unable to send an alarm to anyone. I chewed my bottom lip and glanced at Ronan.

He pushed himself up from leaning over the camera. "No. Absolutely not. I'm not letting you go out there."

"My job is to keep you safe, Ronan. You heard what he said." I gestured to the people around us. "He and all his goons are going to come in here, wreck the place, and maybe even burn it down with all of us inside it."

"The panic room can withstand fire," Ronan said. He thought for a moment before adding, "I think. That's never been tested, and I don't remember what the architect told me. I have the brochure around here somewhere."

I sighed. "What if the only way to save you all is for me to go out there and face whatever Vaughn has in store for me?"

"You know he's going to kill you, right?" Sam raised an eyebrow. "Probably painfully and slowly. Not a good way to go. I'm with Ronan on this one. We're not letting you go out there to certain death."

David and Ryan wisely remained quiet.

"If it comes down to it, it won't be your choice to make. It's mine. But for now, let's follow the protocol that was put in place for exactly this sort of situation." I pressed the big red button on the wall, opening the passage to the panic room.

Ronan frowned. "The panic room? Are you sure?"

I glanced around. There was only one entrance to the security room. Maybe we could hold that position, or maybe we couldn't. I didn't want to risk their lives on a maybe. It would be tight, but it was our only chance.

"Everyone, go," I ordered. "I'm calling for help."

I retrieved my cell phone from the desk where I'd left it before heading to winter but couldn't get signal. They'd jammed us again. Possibly the landline in the panic room was working, and we'd be safe in there in any case. Safer than in the security room, anyway.

I paused at the entrance to the panic room and glanced at the gun safe, considering grabbing some weapons to add to what David and Ryan carried. In the time it'd take me to open the safe, Vaughn would be through the front door, though. Our three minutes were ticking to a close, and we needed to be behind the secondary door before they did. Besides, if it came down to fighting, it would be unlikely that three of us could overpower Vaughn's forces. Sam and Ronan weren't fighters, and I was sore and exhausted, having just come out of another battle. The few precious minutes of sleep I'd gotten in the barracks hadn't been enough.

I entered the stairway, sealing the door behind me.

Stairs descended into a small twelve by twelve room in the sub-basement, insulated against heat and cold. There was supposed to be enough food and water down for two people for two weeks, a phone to call out, and an emergency internet connectivity device.

Ronan ducked through the opening first, descending down the narrow, spiraling stairs. I made sure Sam went in next, then David and Ryan, and I took up the rear. Once I was on the other side of the door, I slammed the red button on that side, closing the door and sealing us inside. Pushing that button also would have silently alerted the police to come and check on the house, starting that timer. Hopefully, they'd get here in time to catch Vaughn in the act and arrest him, although I had to consider the consequences of calling them to the fight. Vaughn was better outfitted than the city cops. His people could take them out, causing further loss of life. I didn't want that blood on my hands, but what choice did I have?

At the bottom of the stairs, I squinted as I stepped into the brightly lit white room. The panic room wasn't anything fancy, minimally outfitted as it was with a few air mattresses, some camping furniture, and those emergency foil blankets. I hoped we wouldn't have to spend the night in there, but that was a worst-case scenario. Even if Vaughn and his people hurt the cops who came to our rescue, the city would send backup. I supposed a true worst-case scenario would be a standoff. That was the only situation where I could see us being stuck down there for days.

The worst part of the panic room was the toilet. It was one of those compostable toilets, and there was limited privacy due to the small space. We had a small folding screen we could put up, but that was about it. If we were stuck down there for very long, it'd be awfully cramped, uncomfortable, and probably start to smell after a short while.

"The police have been notified," I announced as I stepped into the room. "Hopefully they come quickly, and this is all just a speed bump on our way to a nice, relaxing few days." I double-checked that the secondary door was closed and sealed and the vents were working properly, then checked the landline, which was also dead.

David started getting us on the internet as heavy boots stomped across the floors above, the sound distant and muffled thanks to there being a few floors and a lot of insulation between them and us. They had to be making a hell of a lot of noise for us to hear them where we were. There were no cameras down here, so we could only guess what was happening.

We waited, practically holding our breath as we listened to them move around.

It wasn't long before they made their way to the security room, which was the only way they could communicate with us directly. There was an intercom button there that broadcasted through the entire house.

Vaughn found the intercom button. "If you're counting on the police to come and save you, I have bad news for you," he said smugly. "Did you know that most security professionals make just above minimum wage? It's very easy to bribe someone who doesn't know what their time is worth. Slip the local security guy a few thousand dollars, and they were more than happy to come out and disconnect service. I had that done ages ago. So you see, the police won't be getting your call, nor are any of your backup security protocols in place. The house you believed to be a fortress has become your prison."

David shook his head at that point: no internet either.

I turned to Ronan. "A portal. What about making a portal? We could go into Faerie and then come back and surprise him."

Ronan shook his head. "To be a truly useful safe room, it had to be sealed against magic too. There's no way to make a portal in here."

"Great," I said, throwing my hands in the air and plopping down. "Then I guess all that's left to do is sit here and wait to die."

"It's okay, Callie," Ronan said, coming to my side. He put a comforting hand on my back. "We'll be okay. This room can withstand almost everything short of a nuclear bomb."

"The room can," I said, rubbing my temples, "but there are other things he can do to force us out." I pointed to the air vents near the ceiling.

That far below ground and in a sealed room, we had to

rely on a system pumping air into it. If Vaughn found the generator responsible for moving fresh, breathable air into the panic room and shut it off, we'd suffocate within hours, maybe faster. He could also pump gas through it instead, knocking us out, or even killing us.

Also, it might've seemed like we were safely below ground and out of reach, but there were only two doors between Vaughn and us. Granted, they were big metal doors made from some sort of fae alloy, but with the right tools, he could remove them or break them down. He just needed time. Since no police were coming to interrupt him, he had all the time in the world unless we could find a way out.

Whoever had thought up the idea of panic rooms needed to be drawn and quartered. They weren't safe. This place was a death trap.

"I'm sure we'll think of something." Sam sat down on the floor next to me, folding their arms around their knees. "There has to be something in here that can help."

I nodded but didn't have the heart to tell either of them what I really thought. Eventually, Vaughn was going to get what he wanted. I'd have to go out there and face him, leaving the four of them on their own. The best thing I could do was try to negotiate with Vaughn to get him to make a binding promise to leave Ronan and Sam and the guards alone.

Vaughn would find a way to force the issue, or supplies would run out, and when they did, I'd have to make the hard decision to give myself up so they could be safe. That was the job when you were a bodyguard. It was what I'd signed up for.

Since there was nothing else to fill my time with except worrying, I decided to take an inventory of the stock. I'd already seen we had plenty of canned goods, although there was a weird mix of things that didn't go together. I also couldn't find a can opener, which meant they were useless. Note to self: when planning for an apocalyptic situation, always bring a can opener.

There were supposed to be other dry goods down here too that didn't require any preparation or cooking, packaged things like crackers, cookies, and chips. However, no matter how hard I looked, I couldn't find any of them. I pushed aside cans and tried to flatten myself so I could crawl into the shelving. Maybe they'd gotten shoved way back. They were deep shelves, after all.

"What are you doing?" Sam asked from behind me.

"Looking for food," I replied. "There are supposed to be more packaged goods down here. Have you seen any cookies or chips or—" I stopped speaking abruptly as something crunched behind me. When I turned around, I found Sam holding a bag of crinkle-cut potato chips.

"What?" they said, their mouth still full. "I was hungry. Stress makes me hungry."

"What happened to the rest of the dry goods, Sam?"

They swallowed. "Well, um, when you and Ronan left to go to Faerie? I might or might not have come down here to check the place out, spotted all the junk food, and indulged while I had my movie marathon."

I crossed my arms. "So, you're telling me you ate our emergency food, Sam? Two weeks' worth?"

Sam cringed. "In my defense, the fridge was empty, and

all I could find in the kitchen cupboards was some rice and a weird muscle shake mix, so…"

"Sam!" I threw my hands in the air. "Are you kidding me? What happens if we're stuck down here for an extended period?"

"I meant to replace it!" Sam shouted back. "It wasn't like I knew the vampires were going to follow you home, Callie. Although I should've known. You're always bringing trouble around." As soon as Sam said it, their eyes widened, and they put their hands over their mouth.

All the anger I felt drifted away, replaced by a pain in my gut as if a mule had kicked me in the ribs. "Is that really what you think of me, Sam?"

"Callie, I'm sorry. I didn't mean that. It just slipped out."

"We're all under a lot of stress," Ronan said, coming over to where we were. "Maybe it's best if we focus on solving the problem instead of blaming each other. Sam ate the food. That was wrong, they know that, but shouting at them isn't going to change it."

I crossed my arms and turned away. I wasn't even upset over the missing food anymore. What Sam had said cut deep. I already felt like I was a trouble magnet. Hearing them voice that thought hurt.

"I'm sorry," Sam said again. "Ronan's right. It's just the stress of all this, Callie. It's really getting to me. We've been through a lot over the last few months, and it's been exciting and fun sometimes, but this? I'm scared."

I sighed and reached out to put a hand on Sam's shoulder. "I know you are. We all are. But we're going to get through this. Let's go through what's left and see what we can salvage."

Sam handed over the mostly full bag of potato chips. I folded the bag over and placed it on the shelf next to a box of Twinkies. We had chips and Twinkies to keep us going until whenever we could get out of there, not the best diet for a stressful situation. At least there was plenty of bottled water.

Going through some of the drawers, we found a flimsy can opener. It wasn't the greatest, but it would do in a pinch. We also found a hot plate and a very small saucepan. That would make it possible to cook and eat the canned foods on the shelf, which should get us through however long we needed.

Now all that was left was addressing the boredom.

I don't know if you've ever been stuck in a small space for hours on end with two of your favorite people in the world and two you don't know very well, but it can get awfully boring. I was tired, too tired for conversation, but with the vampires wrecking things above us, I didn't think I'd get any sleep. Just to have something to do, I set up the two cots we had and spent the next hour rearranging them in different formations. Everyone wisely stayed out of the way.

Then Sam and I got out the mylar blankets and relieved some of the tension between us by building a blanket fort. It didn't feel any safer inside it, though. While Sam hid inside the blanket fort, I took up a position near the door so I could listen to the vampires moving around the security room above us.

"So," Ronan asked, leaning against the wall beside me, "What is the plan?"

"I'm going to have to go out there," I said.

"Callie..."

"No, I'm serious. It's the only way. We have to get a message out sooner or later, right? Just sitting in here, we're not accomplishing anything. We need to take the fight to the vampires. Leaving the panic room is the only way to do that. What do you think is going to happen when the next shift of security guards shows up, Ronan? You think Vaughn's just going to tell them to turn around and go home? And do you think they'll do it?"

He lowered his head and gripped his side where he'd been injured in the fight in Faerie. "Okay. You're the expert. What do we do?"

"For now, we wait. We have a little time. I'm going to move the phones around. Maybe we can get a signal to send out a text or something. Or maybe Vaughn will screw up. It's too early to tell. They're waiting for us to lose our nerve. I think we'll have a better chance of taking them if we wait just a little bit and have them let their guard down."

Ronan nodded and paced away to sit on one of the cots, satisfied by my answer. I wasn't happy with the answer I'd given him, but it was the only one I could think of. Eventually, we were going to run out of supplies, then we'd be looking at fighting our way out exhausted and weak. It was better to go now before Vaughn brought more people in and strengthened his position, but I needed to think about how we'd do it. I was working on a plan in my head, but I needed time to put it together. When I did, I was going to make Vaughn pay for every minute I'd had to spend down here.

CHAPTER TWENTY-FOUR

I took my cell phone around the panic room, looking for a signal. When that didn't work, I did the same with the other four phones. There wasn't anywhere in the panic room that any of the phones would pick up a signal. I had a single bar for a minute on Sam's phone, but it quickly faded. Vaughn's jamming might not reach here, but we had no signal either? Of course, there was also a landline and a separate internet down here, but Vaughn's people had disabled those too, which wasn't supposed to be possible.

Since the phones were a bust, I turned my attention to coming up with another plan. Ronan and I joined Sam in their crowded blanket fort. David and Ryan just stayed out of the way with their eyes closed.

I found a marker in the supplies and used it to draw out a rough sketch of the house on one of the mylar blankets. We spent the next few hours listening to Vaughn's people move back and forth, trying to determine if they had set up regular patrols. It didn't seem like there was any pattern to the footsteps we heard, which were few and far between.

After that, we decided to pool our resources, laying out everything we had that could be used as a weapon in case we needed to fight our way out, which seemed increasingly likely. I'd left my sword in Faerie, and all my guns were empty of bullets, but I did have one very dull knife. David and Ryan had their guns and several spare mags, and I appropriated one of them and two mags.

We stripped the shoestrings from our shoes. In a pinch, those could be used to strangle someone, although that would require getting much closer than I cared to get to a hostile vampire. Ronan had a belt that was much better for that purpose. There wasn't any body armor in the panic room, but we were able to pull the canvas off the cots and fashion makeshift armor for me. There wasn't enough to do it for the other guards, and they agreed that I'd be doing the majority of the fighting if we broke out of there. Because they had no armor of any kind, during the initial part of the plan, David and Ryan would stay down here.

Sam tore a strip of duct tape off the roll with their teeth and used it to secure some of the canvas to my side. "How many do you think there are?"

"A dozen," I answered. I thought there were a lot more than twelve vampires pacing around the mansion above our head, but I didn't want Sam and Ronan to worry about me.

Ronan crossed his arms, looking on with a frown. "And you think you can take them all?"

I shook my head. "I think I can take one or two if I have to, although if this goes as planned, I won't have to kill anyone."

My plan was to sneak back up the stairs, sealing the

panic room door behind me. Maybe I could get cell signal in the stairway, but I doubted it. I had to try, though, just in case.

If not, I'd go into the security room and fight my way through the vampires that were there if I had to, or sneak by if I could. If I was lucky, I'd be able to sneak down to the basement or to a window where I could climb out and make a call for help from safety. There were too many vampires for the three professionals to fight them off, poorly armed as we were. If I could liberate the security room above, though, we would have access to all the guns and armor we needed. The problem was, the fight would make a lot of noise, which would draw more vampires. Fighting for the security room was Plan C, right after me somehow managing to sneak out of the house. I didn't like leaving Ronan and Sam in the panic room, even with David and Ryan there with one of the guns, but I had a better chance of calling for help if I went on alone. Three people sneaking through the house would make more noise than one.

"What if Vaughn is in the security room?" Ronan asked.

I ground my teeth. I should've killed him a long time ago and saved us all the headache. If I saw him now, I'd be tempted to take him out just to make sure he didn't come after us again, but I could restrain myself. "So what if he is?"

"Then what?" Ronan shrugged. "You don't think we should just take him out and get it over with?"

Sam peeled more tape from the roll and pressed it to my arm, circling it around. "You mean, cut off the head of the snake."

"That's not how it works," I explained. "Vaughn is smart. Even though he's charismatic and their leader, the others aren't going to stop fighting just because we killed their boss. There will be other people under him to give commands. As long as there are more than two of them, someone will step up to make decisions and give orders. We won't be able to end this just by killing one man, as tempting as it sounds."

"Damn," Sam muttered. "I kind of want him to die."

"You're not the only one," I muttered.

Sam finished taping the cot canvas to me. I felt like a walking version of the Michelin man. The canvas wasn't meant for that purpose, meaning it didn't give much when I walked. I was starting to think I'd have been better off just wrapping myself in duct tape. Maybe I should have Sam go all over me with that roll one more time. You could never have too much duct tape, after all.

But no amount of canvas or duct tape was going to stop bullets. At best, I was geared up to keep from being bitten or stabbed. If they pulled a gun on me, I'd be as screwed as usual.

I waddled away from Sam to the center of the panic room, turning an awkward circle. "How do I look?"

"Like a very confused cot maker," Ronan said, nodding. "Are you sure all this was necessary?"

David and Ryan just shook their heads.

"Anything that protects me from getting bitten by a vampire helps." I flexed my arms and legs, trying to get the canvas to cooperate. It was noisy as hell, crinkling with every move. The vampires would hear me for sure. I sighed. "Maybe this was a bad idea." Before anyone could answer me, the constant whirring that had filled the room suddenly died. The silence that followed was oddly uneasy. I looked around. "What the hell was that?"

"The ventilation fans." Ronan put his hand in front of one of the vents.

I cursed. "I was wondering when they'd figure out how to shut those off. How much air do you think we have down here?"

Sam mumbled some math. "An hour? Maybe two. Not long. Depends on how many breaths per minute we're taking."

We all stared at Sam.

"What?" They shrugged. "I might be an art major, but I had to take algebra!"

"Okay, fine." I started to peel off the duct tape and the makeshift canvas armor.

"What are you doing?" Sam tugged their hair, aghast that I was destroying all their hard work.

"We have to get out of here, and sneaking around in this isn't going to make that happen." I yanked the last of the duct tape off my arm, wincing as it pulled away all the hair. "He wants me, he can have me. I'm going up there."

"Callie, we discussed this." Ronan put a hand on my shoulder. "He's going to kill you. I won't let that happen."

"Would you rather all five of us die?" I gestured around the room. "Look, I have no intention of letting Vaughn kill me. I'm going to make it as difficult as possible for him. But hiding down here is a death sentence. Our best chance of making it out of this alive rests in me going up there. I'm going to talk through the upper door to him and see if we can't come to some sort of agreement."

"Callie—"

"Ronan. Trust me."

He sighed and relented with a nod, stepping aside. "Okay. You're the expert. I trust you."

"Thank you," I said and went to the panic room door, punching in the code to open it. "Close this behind me, and don't open it until I tell you. Understand?"

They agreed.

The air in the panic room was already growing a little stale, enough so that when I opened the door to the stairway, it was easier to breathe. Maybe it was all in my head, or maybe they had less time than Sam thought.

I made my way as slowly and silently as I could to the locked door at the top. It too was sealed from my side. Vaughn wouldn't be able to open it, not without anything short of a concentrated blast that would blow up half the house and alert the whole neighborhood. I could hear vampires scurrying around on the other side, moving back and forth. Goodness knew what they were doing. I checked for signal, but still no dice. There went Plans A and B. On to Plan C.

The room beyond went deathly silent when I knocked on the door three times. "Listen up, bloodsuckers! This is Callie Hart. I demand to speak with Vaughn right now."

Feet shuffled closer. "You're hardly in any position to make demands," said Vaughn through the door. His voice was muffled, but I was sure it was him.

Dammit. It was exactly as I thought; they'd set up their base of operations in the security room, which meant it was crawling with vampires.

"If that were true, you wouldn't be talking to me," I

answered. "What is it you want? Besides me, I mean. I get that. You want revenge because I screwed up your plans, but why go through all this? You could've grabbed me anywhere."

"Because you think this house is a fortress. Because you think you're safe and untouchable. It sends a message, don't you see? If I can take you here, I can do it anywhere."

"So, you're telling me this is about saving your reputation after you got your ass handed to you in Faerie?" I laughed. "Give me a break."

"You're the one who wanted to speak to me, Callie. I'm perfectly content to sit up here and let the five of you suffocate. Or you can open that door and we can settle this, you and me."

I sat down, my back to the door. "You don't want to kill us. Imagine if you did. Mab and Titania are already hunting you. If you killed Ronan, they'd burn everything you ever touched to the ground. They'd erase your legacy and your name from history. There wouldn't even be enough of you to bury. No, you want me to negotiate because you're smarter than that. You know Ronan's more valuable to you alive than dead. Sam's nothing to you, though, and the guards aren't even a threat. Can we at least agree to let them and Sam go?"

"I bear your friend no ill will. If you open the door, Sam will be free to go. The guards, too," Vaughn promised.

I waited for further guarantees, but when none came, I had to force the issue. "And Ronan? What about him?"

"As you said, Ronan is a valuable political prisoner. I can use him to bargain with Mab, perhaps even force her to call her dogs off and let me be. With him, I might be able to salvage some of my victory. You, however, cannot be allowed to live. Open the door, Callie, and surrender. I will take Ronan prisoner, negotiate with Mab, and let the others go free. The only blood I demand is yours. Think of it as a final act of self-sacrifice for the man you love."

A cold chill ran down my spine. Something about the way he said that told me he was lying. I knew he was. There was nothing Vaughn could do or say to convince me he meant no harm to Sam or Ronan, but what choice did I have? If I didn't open the door, they'd be dead in a few hours anyway.

I had one chance to end this in my favor, and it relied on Vaughn having a shred of honor left in him. "What about a duel?"

He was silent for a moment before repeating, "A duel?"

"You know, you and I fight to the death. Everyone else stays out of it. The winner takes all. If I win, everybody down there goes free and your people leave, and I agree not to tell Mab about any of this. If you win, you let Sam and the guards go and guarantee Ronan lives."

Vaughn considered it for a long moment. I could practically hear the wheels turning in his head on the other side of the door. He just needed a little push to convince him. Unfortunately, I could also hear one of his lackeys on the other side, explaining to him why it was such a bad idea.

"She's basically a human girl," Vaughn spat. "How difficult can she be to kill?"

"We've tried before," said the lackey.

"You have, but I haven't."

"Come on, Vaughn," I pushed. "You going to let your underlings tell you what to do? Don't you want the chance to prove you've got bigger balls than a woman in front of all your men?"

"Fine," Vaughn snapped. "If you want a duel, I'm happy to give you one, though it will only be prolonging the inevitable. I agree to your terms, Callie. Now open the door."

I bit my lip. Moment of truth. Vaughn could still betray me and decide he'd rather kill us all than keep his word. Part of me fully expected him to. Vaughn wasn't famous for his honor. I'd had to practically emasculate the guy to get him to agree to the duel. Honestly, that had probably worked better than anything else I could've tried. The way he saw it, he had everything to lose if he didn't fight me. At least, I hoped so.

I typed the code into the number pad beside the door, letting my finger hover over the last digit. There was still time to change my mind, but then what? What other option was there but to open that door? Let four trapped people suffocate slowly? Anything was better than watching my friends die horribly.

I finished punching in the code. The door slid open.

The barrels of three machine guns were leveled at my face as Vaughn's lackeys closed in. I put my hands up, showing I wasn't armed. They yanked me out of the stairway, pushed me against the wall, and patted me down. They found the gun and discarded it and the mags.

"Open the other door," Vaughn commanded. "And take them to the kitchen. Bind them to the house they tried so desperately to hide behind and let them burn with it."

"You son of a bitch!" I spun but didn't get a chance to take a swing at him before his goons grabbed my arms and cuffed my hands behind my back. "I knew you were lying!"

He smiled smugly. "Of course you did, but you couldn't just sit there on the other side of the door completely helpless, could you? That's not what Callie Hart does. She protects people. She acts. It's a pity you've never been much of a thinker. Then again, you were a good soldier. Good at following orders, not so good at thinking on her own." He jerked his head to the side. "Take them."

They didn't know the code, I thought. There was still hope.

As I looked over my shoulder, I saw one of Vaughn's vampires shining a blacklight over the keypad that showed which buttons I'd pressed to open the upper door. Since they were on the same system, the code was the same for both. It'd only be a matter of time before they got the second door open.

Well, I thought as they dragged me toward the kitchen, at least they won't suffocate in that tiny room.

I fought them as they carried me down the stairs, managing to break free of my escorts for a minute. I lost my footing on the stairs, though, and would have fallen face-first down them and probably broken my neck at the bottom if they hadn't grabbed me.

Now what? How are you going to get out of this one, Callie? No one is coming to save you. You're unarmed and facing being burned alive, which isn't any better than the suffocation you were staring down a few minutes ago. To say things had gone from bad to worse was an understatement.

But the situation wasn't hopeless. Vaughn had forgotten one very important fact. He could burn the place down and set everything on fire, but if I could get my magic to work, it'd all be for nothing. Now that I wasn't trapped in that sealed room, there was nothing stopping me from letting all hell break loose. Nothing except the ties they had on my wrists.

CHAPTER TWENTY-FIVE

As ordered, the vampires took me to the kitchen and plopped me down in one of the chairs, securing me to it with more plastic zip-ties. I tested their strength and found they'd put them on correctly. I wouldn't be breaking them anytime soon.

I wasn't alone in the room for long. A few minutes after they'd secured me to my chair, the vampires brought in Ronan and Sam and David and Ryan. My heart sank at the sight of them. I had known they would be coming because Vaughn had obviously lied to me, but seeing them made it more real. Sam fought the vampires dragging them by the hair, trying fruitlessly to land a kick. The vamps picked Sam up with ease, held them down, and zip-tied both of Sam's wrists to the back of the chair. Ronan and the guards didn't bother. They knew as well as I did that there was no point in wasting energy on fighting at this stage. We'd need that for what came next.

"Are you four okay?" I asked once they'd been seated and tied to their chairs.

The vampires grabbed each of our chairs and spun them around, scooting them so that the five of us were in a rough circle.

"Considering what?" Ronan's voice was still strangely upbeat. "I'm in one piece and still breathing. I guess that means I'm okay for now."

"Not for long," said one of the vampires. The other let out a hissing chuckle. They left the room, laughing to themselves.

Sam twisted. I could just barely make out their profile off to my left and Ronan's to my right. "What are they going to do?"

"If Vaughn lives up to his word, I think they're going to burn the place down with us inside," I answered.

Ronan sighed.

"What?" I twisted toward him.

"Nothing. I was trying to remember if my homeowner's insurance policy protected against vampires burning the house down."

If I could have seen his face, I would have stared at him in disbelief. "Here we are, tied to chairs and facing burning alive, and all you can think about is if your insurance will pay for the damages?"

His shoulder lifted slightly in a shrug. "I'm trying to stay positive and believe we're going to get out of this. Somehow."

The vampires came back in with big red cans of gasoline, dumping it in a circle around us. The smell stung my nose and eyes and I turned my head away, choking on the fumes. They soaked the floor of the kitchen, the table, and the appliances.

Vaughn came in behind them, his hands folded behind his back and a smug smile fixed on his face. "A pity it came to this," he said, stopping just short of stepping in the gasoline spreading over the floor. "You could've died on your feet. Instead, I've had to resort to this. Oh, don't struggle. And don't reach for your magic either. Those aren't normal zip-ties around your wrists. I've made sure you won't be able to call ice to stop these flames. As you can see, Callie, I'm prepared for everything. I know everything you're going to do before you do."

The goons emptied the gasoline cans and walked up to him. "Should we light it now, boss?"

Vaughn's grin grew larger. "Not yet. First, let's make sure all that will be left is rubble. Tear down what you can. Burn the rest." He turned his back and walked out of the room.

The vampires stepped out too, only to return with sledgehammers and crowbars. I flinched as they pried cabinets off the wall and smashed the marble countertop. They broke the glass on the oven door, bashed the table into splinters, and broke what was left of the dishes before pausing to spit on us. Then they moved on to the rest of the house. We sat, listening to them tear apart what was left of Ronan's beautiful house.

I struggled against the ties around my wrists and reached for my magic. True to Vaughn's words, I could feel it lurking just out of reach, and it wouldn't answer my call when I tried to coax it forward. Inside, a part of me panicked, but I pushed that part down with steady breathing. Panic wouldn't help us now. I needed a clear head and to stay focused. If the ties were the problem, I needed to remove them. Problem was, I couldn't snap them given the way they were positioned, but the vampires had used plastic ties. With enough effort, I could stretch them and wiggle free. I started twisting my wrists, pulling against the ties as hard as I could and releasing repeatedly. Eventually, it would work. I just didn't know if it would be before we died.

"Callie," Ronan said.

"Not now." I pulled again on the plastic restraints. *Come on, you pieces of crap. Break!*

"Listen to me, Callie."

"Dammit, Ronan, I said, not now. I'm trying to break these."

"Good luck." Sam snorted. "I watched this documentary once where they tested how to do that, and they concluded that the worst possible scenario was exactly the one we're in so… Yeah. Good luck."

I rolled my eyes. "Not helping, Sam."

"I'm sorry, but this can't wait," Ronan said more insistently. "I don't want to die leaving things unsaid, and with the way this is going, I need to get it out in the open so we can stop dancing around it like idiots." He took a deep breath. "I'm in love with you."

I stopped struggling against the restraints. "Really? Now?"

"Well, it doesn't look like we're going to live much longer, so I figured now was the best time."

I let out a frustrated growl. "Now is the worst time, Ronan!"

"I think it's sweet," Sam said. "Downright adorable. And you two would have made a lovely couple."

Ronan nodded. "Thank you, Sam."

"You're forgetting something." I grunted as I fought the tensile strength of the plastic zip-ties. I could swear I felt it give a little more each time. "I'm still your head of security."

"Oh, screw the job," Ronan spat. "I'll get someone else. Hell, I'll go without a bodyguard if I have to. Maybe I'll defend myself."

I almost laughed at the thought, imagining him throwing drumsticks at a would-be attacker and flinging other instruments around. Ronan wasn't much of a fighter. "Come on, Ronan."

He kept going. "I don't care if I lose this house, my position at court, favor with Mab, or anything. I can lose everything, Callie, but I can't lose you. Not now that I know you. I can't imagine my life without you in it, and I don't want to. I need you with me, Callie."

"I need to get out of these damn restraints!" I gave them one last pull before collapsing against the back of the chair, exhausted. It was no use. No matter how hard I pulled, they just wouldn't loosen enough for me to slip one hand free. We were doomed.

"Say something," Ronan urged.

I sat there in silence. The vampires were still busting up whatever they wanted and smashing all the glass. It was only a matter of time before they got bored with breaking the last few things and started the fire. Vaughn would probably sit on the front lawn, roasting marshmallows over the ashes until the fire department eventually showed up. Who knew how long that would take? We'd have to wait for the neighbors to see the smoke and be bothered enough by it to take action.

"Callie?" Ronan pushed.

"I'm thinking."

The front door swung open. I recognized the sound of it on its hinges. A lighter was struck, and something small fell to the floor with a quiet *thud*. A moment later, fire raced into the kitchen, curling around and streaking through the gasoline in bright blue flames. The heat and the burning fumes stung. I closed my eyes, turning my face away. This was it. This was how I was going to die—helpless and tied to a chair. Not how I'd pictured my death.

I tried to take a breath and choked on it. That little panicked voice I'd pushed out of the forefront of my mind reared its ugly head again, and this time I had no choice but to acknowledge it. This was real. I was staring death in the face, closer than I'd probably ever been, with no path to surviving. Not just me but Sam and Ronan and David and Ryan too. God, what if one of them went first? I'd have to sit next to them and listen to it happen. That would be worse than dying myself.

I squeezed my eyes shut. Tears leaked out, trailing down my cheeks. The smoke and heat made my nose run.

"All right!" I shouted, no longer willing to hold back. "If we're going to die, I might as well get it out. I have feelings for you too, Ronan."

"Really?" he choked out and coughed.

"Yeah, and by the way, this job sucks. I quit!"

"Um, Callie?" Sam's chair scooted back slightly, away from the fire. "What do we do?"

I could hear the fear in their voice, a real and genuine

terror I'd never heard before. Sam's voice wasn't supposed to sound like that. They were supposed to be happy, even hyper. It sounded wrong. Something about hearing the panic and fear in Sam's voice sent me over the edge. My own fear faded to nothing.

"Screw this," I muttered and closed my eyes. I was going to call my power or die trying.

The flames rose, the heat increasing, burning the air until breathing it made my lungs and throat raw. The fire crackled as it devoured the wooden debris in the room. Black smoke rose, gathering at the ceiling like a sentient being, waiting, thickening, and eating all the oxygen, slowly growing large enough to block out everything else.

I was aware of it all, but I was also working diligently to shut it out. All sensory input became nothing more than a distraction. The only thing that mattered was reaching my magic, coaxing it through any narrow holes I could find in the spelled zip-tie, threading it to my fingers, and sending it out to stop the fire. As I searched for my power, the world came into sharper focus. I could smell Ronan's sweat, Sam's perfume, and the burning wood glue that was on the cabinets somewhere. Underneath it all was the stink of gasoline and vampires all over the house.

Every fear surfaced at once: the fear of dying, fear of pain, fear of the unknown that waited beyond life, fear of failing my friends. I grabbed those fears and funneled them like energy into my efforts to reach my magic, and as the power swelled, the ties on my wrists snapped and fell away. I stretched my palms forward, blasting the area where the fire and smoke were thickest with as much ice as I could muster. Frost crawled up the walls, calming the black storm of smoke. Flames died with a hiss as the ice melted, then froze a second time.

I rose from my chair and sent another wave of cold magic out over everything, coating the fire in ice. The fire in the kitchen died to embers. With a shout of effort, I sent another stream of ice into the hallway, first on one side, then the other. I willed it to keep going, keep growing, expanding over what was left of the whole house until there was no more fire.

When my magic was spent, I staggered on my feet and fell into a hot puddle. Ice dripped onto my face from the melting icicles on the ceiling.

"Callie!" Ronan called, but his voice seemed far away.

I could barely stay awake, I was so tired. The magic had taken the last of my energy and I needed a minute to recover. If I could just close my eyes...

No. I forced my eyes back open. Sam and Ronan and the others needed me.

Slowly, I rolled onto my stomach and pushed myself up with a grunt. My limbs ached as if I'd just had the workout of a lifetime. I hadn't hurt that bad since boot camp. I did my best to shake it off and limped over to where the knives lay under an inch of water on the floor. My vision blurred as I reached for one. I shook my head clear, picked up the knife, and returned to cut Sam free first. They jumped up and squeezed me.

"I'm okay," I assured them, patting their back. "I just need to get Ronan and the others free." I pushed the chairs aside and slid the knife under the zip-ties holding Ronan's hands in place. They snapped under the slight pressure and fell into the water. I stared at them floating there, amazed that such small things had almost gotten us all killed.

Ronan stood, rubbing his wrists, as I freed David and Ryan. Ronan turned, threw the chair aside, and took my face in his hands. The first kiss in Faerie had been so brief it barely counted, but this one… There was no doubt in my mind that it counted. Suddenly, the pain didn't matter. The exhaustion faded, and all that mattered was being there with him, alive and in the moment.

Then I heard the click of a gun.

I opened my eyes wide and stepped back. Ronan had frozen because Vaughn stood behind him, a gun pressed to the back of his head. The bastard had snuck up on us. In an instant, he could pull that trigger, and Ronan would be dead. There was nothing I could do to stop him.

Slowly, I raised my hands in surrender. David and Ryan had left as soon as they were free. I hoped they were still alive, but they were definitely fired.

"Move," Vaughn spat, "and he dies. Honestly, I should kill him anyway, shouldn't I? This has gone far enough. I don't know how you got free and I don't care, but I am tired of being shown up by some half-breed girl whose only qualification for her job is being in the right place at the right time." He shifted the gun, pointing it at me. "It appears that if you want something done right, you really do have to do it yourself." His finger tightened on the trigger.

Ronan turned into Vaughn, knocking him off balance. I ducked at the same moment. The gun went off, but the shot hit the ceiling since Ronan had tackled Vaughn to the floor. He twisted the gun away from the vampire and punched him in the face. Vaughn hissed, showed his fangs, and latched onto Ronan's outstretched arm, biting deep.

The knife, I thought, looking around. I'd just had one of the kitchen knives in my hand, and that would be perfect for staking a vampire. I fell to my hands and knees, sliding my palms through the melting ice, searching for the knife while Vaughn and Ronan wrestled and punched each other.

Vaughn finally managed to get Ronan off him, throwing him against the refrigerator. Ronan bounced off the door and landed on the floor, leaving a big dent behind. The door swung open slightly. Vaughn picked Ronan up by the throat and slammed him again against the fridge. This time when he pulled him away, the contents spilled out into the inch or so of water on the floor.

Vaughn held Ronan by the throat against the wall next to the fridge, his fist drawn back. "I should've killed you a long time ago."

My hand closed around a stainless steel handle. Bingo— I'd found the knife. I picked it up and charged at Vaughn. He jerked as the knife went into his back, straight through his ribcage and into his heart from behind. Slowly, his fingers released Ronan and let him fall to the floor. Vaughn staggered back a step and tried to turn, but he exploded into dust before he could complete the movement.

Sam came running back into the kitchen with a battle cry, holding a plunger. They stopped after a few steps and looked around. "Damn, did I miss it?"

"It's over," I confirmed and extended a hand to Ronan. "Vaughn is finally dead."

CHAPTER TWENTY-SIX

Although the magic had put out the fire, parts of the house had been badly burned. It still smoldered in some areas, and the stairs didn't look structurally sound. I decided it would be safer for everyone to go outside, where we'd call the fire department.

On our way out, we stopped by the library and Ronan glanced inside, breathing a sigh of relief when he saw that most of his books were untouched by the fire somehow. I guess the vampires hadn't doused them with gasoline. Everything from the third shelf up was just the way he'd left it, meaning he'd only lost about a third of the books he never seemed to find the time to read.

The rest of the house, though, looked like a total loss. Maybe we'd need to have a look at his homeowner's policy after all.

The fire department showed up on their own shortly after I ushered everybody outside. One of the neighbors must've seen the smoke and called for help. If only they'd called an hour or two sooner, the house might still be in livable condition. Burned and flooded as it was, I didn't think anyone would be living there anytime soon.

The firefighters walked around, scratching their heads. The fire was obviously arson, so they wanted to bring in an arson investigator, which would take days and hold up the insurance payout for a considerable amount of time. Of course, they'd never find the culprits since they had bolted when Vaughn died.

The fire made sense to them, at least on some level, but they didn't know how to take the melting piles of ice everywhere. I didn't know how to explain it to mundane humans, so I didn't try. Whenever they asked, I shrugged and joked that maybe the air conditioning had been on too high. No one seemed as pleased with the joke as I was, but I kept telling it.

The fire chief, the arson investigator, and the police wanted to interview the three of us, but that would wait until after they finished making sure all the fires were out inside. In the meantime, Sam, Ronan, and I found a spot on the lawn and sat down in a line, arms folded, watching the regular humans work. They kicked around ash that had once been living beings. Granted, they had been vampires, but it was unsettling to think that they were walking through remains without realizing it.

It was Sam who voiced what we were all thinking first. "So, now what?"

I shrugged. "Now what, what?"

Sam gestured to the house. "Our flat is a mess and about to be torn down. Ronan's mansion is all but destroyed. Half our stuff was in there and is probably wrecked or burned. Where are we going to live, Callie?

And how are we going to replace our clothes and things? As it stands, I don't even have a toothbrush."

"Don't worry about replacing your lost items," Ronan said confidently. "I can cover that and put us all up in a nice hotel for a while too. I have enough set aside, although this will be quite a blow. I had a lot of equity tied up in the house. Mab won't be happy when she hears what happened here. Then again, Vaughn is out of the picture. I'm going to emphasize that when I tell her."

"That money's not going to last forever." I sighed and wrapped my arms around my knees. "Sam has no income when school's out of session, and Ronan, your work is tenuous at best, especially since you didn't show up for your last few gigs."

He cringed. "Yeah, that's going to hurt, but I can still afford dinner and a movie. That is, if you're up for it?" Ronan looked at me with a big grin.

I sighed again, shook my head, and leaned against his shoulder. "Is it too late to take back that I quit? I have a feeling I'm going to need a viable income source. Will you still be able to afford me? That's the question. I want a raise after all this."

Ronan laughed. "I'm not hard up for cash just yet, and don't forget that you're on Mab's good side now. You've done such a good job, I'm sure she'll want me to keep you on. I won't be running out of money anytime soon.

"We could always start a detective agency," Sam piped up, sitting up straighter. "Callie can be the muscle, I'll be the brains, and Ronan can be…" They rolled their hand, trying to think of a role for him to play. "You can be the

Pierce Brosnan guy. You know, the one who was James Bond in the nineties?"

"You mean the pretty boy who reels in all the clients?" I said.

Sam snapped their fighters. "Right! That!"

Ronan smiled and laughed. "Well, I do look very good in suits, although I show less skin."

I rolled my eyes and fell back against the grass, looking up at the smoke-filled sky. "Give me a break. You've always been more of a *Moonlighting* guy."

He shrugged. "Maybe. Either way, it'd be fun. Sam does have a point. You're more than qualified, and I'm in a position to finance a venture without any financial strain. We could do some real good for the community. Help people." He eyed the house. "Although maybe we should refrain from burning down any more property."

I laid there on my back, staring at the sky with my hands folded over my chest while the two of them talked excitedly about how they'd go about founding a detective agency. Apparently, it wasn't all that complicated, and Sam knew people who could help the idea go forward. Of course they did. Sam knew everybody in the human world, and Ronan was connected in Faerie. There was no doubt in my mind that if anybody could get it done, it was the two of them.

As for me, I'd go along with whatever they decided. No matter what the next venture was, it couldn't be as dangerous as being Ronan's bodyguard during a fae-vampire war. I could be the muscle in a detective agency, or just go on being a bodyguard to someone. Actually, I thought I'd make a pretty good private eye, especially now that I understood my powers a little better. With Ronan and Sam helping me, there wasn't much I couldn't do.

It was funny how much things had changed in a few months. It seemed like a lifetime ago that I was just a night security guard, trying to climb the corporate ladder to make a buck. While I hadn't been miserable, I hadn't been happy in that life. I'd had Sam, but even then, I was alone and a workaholic. I might've stayed that way if I hadn't stumbled on those vampire assassins trying to take out an underwear model in the back room of a factory.

Over the course of a few months, I'd also found out I wasn't as alone in the world as I thought. My mother might've been a half-crazy fae queen, but she was alive and had been reasonable about half the times we'd interacted. Not only that, but I had a brother—a twin brother—and I'd found my father. I'd somehow managed to hunt down the family I'd wanted to find, and turned my friends into a family I didn't know I needed.

I guess a stable living situation was a small price to pay for everything I'd gained.

Sam and Ronan leaned over my legs.

I propped myself up on my elbows. "What are you two doing?"

"Looking at rentals near campus," Ronan mumbled. "There are some nice three-bedroom places available with plenty of room for all of us."

The End

If you enjoyed this adventure with Callie Hart, you may also enjoy Bailey Nordin's story in the WereWitch series, also from Renée Jaggér.

If Were tradition forced you to marry at twenty-five, would you do it?

Bailey Nordin is feeling the stress of pack obligations arriving too soon in her life.

She prefers working on cars to going on a date.

A good fight is just a morning's workout, and Bailey's sarcastic wit has killed any chance of a love life.

Her future isn't looking bright.

Roland is on the run from three powerful witches who want him for...*what he can provide.*

Trying to hide from the witches, he ends up in the middle of a town so small, it's hard to find it on a map.

She's a Were, He's a wizard. He could be her ticket out of her problems—if she believed in magic.

Massive changes are coming down from the heavens, and Bailey Nordin is the Were in the middle.

Will she figure out how to break from tradition?

"It's like Romeo and Juliet... A Were and a wizard fighting kidnappers, gods, and a mysterious government agency that is trying to hide the paranormal from society.

You know what? It's actually nothing like Romeo and Juliet.

Except no one wants those two together, especially the witches."

Available at your favorite online book store

You made it! Here we are again at the end book three, the last book in the series. Thank you so much for reading this far.

What does one do when one is full of coffee, had taken enough hikes to wear out one's boots, and even the dog doesn't get excited when one goes near the door anymore?

One works on the garden! During my enforced leisure, I redesigned part of my yard, put in some heirloom roses from an online seller (Zephrine Drouhins are my fave, they smell fabulous), and constructed a water feature out of stock tanks with two waterfalls. Stock tanks since the feed store is still open, Amazon ships pumps and weirs, and Etsy sellers have great water plants. As I imbibed my morning caffeine fix today, I looked over a fabulous garden with mellifluous water sounds right next to my back porch. Roses are already open and smelling great!

Now if I can just keep Jo out of the stock tank long enough for the water lilies to bloom. Looking forward to summer nights with fairy lights in the garden.

Maybe I can make a Zoom background out of it? Hmmm… I'm sure I could find a llama or two somewhere to add interest. Maybe some chickens.

Before I go, I always thank my advance reader team, especially Kelly and Paul, for their thoughtful suggestions and pointing out story issues.

I hope you enjoyed Callie's and Ronan's final adventure. You might have noticed I left a little loophole in the last chapter, so if you like these folks, they *could* come back.

Reviews are the lifeblood of any writer. I hope you leave them for me or any other author whose books you enjoy. We appreciate you!

Until next time,

Renée

PS: Did you know you can grow regular cannas as bog plants? Me either, but they do really well.

I COULDN'T DO THIS WITHOUT YOU!

Thanks to my early readers, you rock!

Misty Roa, Deb Mader, Jim Caplan, Paul Westman, Kerry Mortimer, Debi Sateren, Diane L. Smith

The WereWitch Series
Bad Attitude (Book One)
A Bit Aggressive (Book Two)
Too Much Magic (Book Three)

The Callie Hart Series
Thin Ice
Cold Blood
Feelings Run Deep

www.ingramcontent.com/pod-product-compliance
Lightning Source LLC
Chambersburg PA
CBHW050251110726

47898CB00007B/2365